Carol
for
Another
Christmas

Carol for Another Christmas

ᚙᚙᚙ

ELIZABETH ANN SCARBOROUGH

Ace Books, New York

CAROL FOR ANOTHER CHRISTMAS

An Ace Book
Published by The Berkley Publishing Group
200 Madison Avenue, New York, NY 10016

The Putnam Berkley World Wide Web site address is
http://www.berkley.com/berkley
Make sure to check out PB Plug, the science fiction/fantasy
newsletter, at http://www.pbplug.com

Book design by Irving Perkins Associates

First Edition: November 1996

Library of Congress Cataloging-in-Publication Data

Scarborough, Elizabeth Ann.
    Carol for another Christmas / Elizabeth Ann Scarborough. —
1st ed.
        p.   cm.
    "An Ace book."
    ISBN 0-441-00366-4
    I. Title.
PS3569.C324C37   1996
8313'.54—dc20   96-24754
                                                        CIP

Printed in the United States of America

10 9 8 7 6 5 4 3 2 1

Dedication

❦

For my computer-wise niece and nephew, Cynthia Dawn and Jason Allen Scarborough, Merry Christmas from Aunt Annie

Acknowledgments

⟨∾∾∾⟩

Thanks to Joyce Thompson for sharing her enthusiasm about writers and technology and for introducing me to Miriam Harline and Harald Henry, who shepherded me around Microsoft and introduced me to many lovely, technically gifted people including Jonathan Espenschied and Brian Meyers. Any mistakes along technical lines in this book are my fault, not theirs, and I thank all of them plus others who shared their time and knowledge with me. Also, thanks to Ron Wodaski, my Port Townsend neighbor, for his suggestions. And of course, my most humble gratitude to Charles Dickens for the wonderful tale we all love to listen to, watch, read, and re-create Christmas after Christmas.

Prologue

Ebenezer Scrooge was being haunted again, which was remarkable, since to the best of his recollection, he was already dead.

Everyone had said so. His spirit had lingered a bit while the register of his burial was signed, like that of his partner Marley before him, by the clergyman, the clerk, the undertaker, and the chief mourner. His nephew signed it, weeping. Scrooge noted the tears with feelings that were understandably mixed since, while he was not particularly happy to have departed a life he had only begun to enjoy, it did please him to see that the departure was mourned.

In the five years since he had been visited by the ghosts of Christmas Past, Present, and Future, he had been a changed man, a generous man, and had become—dare he say it?—a beloved man. Everyone had forgotten the past, when he was curmudgeonly, miserly, and mean. Until now, that is. For suddenly, his past had returned to mock him.

"Humbug!" was the word that awakened him. "Humbug!" was what he used to say when asked for charity or when wished a merry Christmas; any time, indeed, when it would have been more appropriate to show a little kindness, a little joy. His answer had been not only "Humbug" but "Bah! Humbug!" and it was the latter word that now returned to haunt him.

A bolt of light seared through him and a single word, "Yes!" resounded triumphantly above the echo of "Humbug."

One

⌇⌇⌇

The morning before Christmas was typically gray and gloomy Seattle winter weather, motorists giving thanks, as they drove off Interstates 5 and 90, that the snow forecast for the day had missed them on their morning commute. Downtown twinkled with white fairy lights and smelled of fir and pine from the many brightly decorated trees throughout town. Christmas flags hung from lampposts. Later in the day, horse-drawn carriages with drivers dressed in Victorian velvet and top hats would rattle and clop through city streets, carrying harried shoppers and high-spirited children. Store windows beckoned with every sort of luxurious gift and piles of beautifully wrapped boxes.

The street people's cups clinked with extra coins and many said "Merry Christmas" as a thank-you, while bracing themselves for a snowy night. Wind pulled at hair and mufflers and turned umbrellas inside out. Vendors sold steaming espresso to shoppers sporting Santa Claus and Christmas tree lapel pins. Street musicians trotted out their Christmas carols and sang and played them on guitars, banjos, accordions, hammered dulcimers, and harmonicas.

But in one large corner of the city, no lights brightened
the cement buildings except the bleak square moons of flou-
rescent-lit office corridor windows. Within the mausoleum,
stillness was broken only by the skeletal clickings of finger-
tips on plastic, while tiny dots of red, green, and yellow light
flickered like the eyes of feral animals. Blue and green
screens full of arcane symbols and letters held the occupants
of the offices enthralled.

The spell was abruptly shattered by the tolling of an elevator bell followed by carpet-padded footsteps striding into
the labyrinth of offices. A hand that might as well have been
clawed lashed out, nails squealing against glass, and ripped
paper. For a moment the office's occupant was held in a
threatening glare accented with Lancome's blue-black mas-
cara from Nordstrom's, and then released as the figure
swooped into the next office.

From keyboard to keyboard the tiny E-mail window
opened and the word spread silently down the hall, "The
Dragonlady is abroad—no sexism intended—beware!"

The footsteps stopped, a door creaked open, and a chair
squealed as weight sank into it. Slowly, reluctantly, the
moonglow screens were abandoned as the shuffling feet of
the office occupants dragged into the conference room.

A woman whose ample curves could have bespoken jollity and generosity had they not settled into a puddle of
rippling discontent sat in the power position behind a great
desk. The white streaks in her hair could have meant she
was wise, except that they corkscrewed like tortured snakes
in all directions. Her face was well made up, which might

have meant that she cared about her appearance to others, but instead it had the appearance of a deceptively rosy, wide-eyed mask. And her neat black suit and crisp poly-blend blouse could have been demure and understated, but rather bore the aspect of full battle dress.

"Now then," she said sweetly, when her employees, like feudal serfs, had filed into the office to stand around her desk. "Can anyone tell me what day this is?"

"It's Christmas Eve," someone muttered.

"Good." She smiled. It did not transform her face in any significant way. "It's Christmas Eve. Brilliant. I'm beginning to believe what I've been told about what high IQs you all have. Now for the toughie. If today is Christmas Eve, what does that make tomorrow?"

"Christmas, Ms. Banks," the employees said like a kindergarten class. Ms. Banks's eyes narrowed a bit as she searched their young faces for any overt signs of mockery. All she saw was the tops of dropped heads, blank expressions, or determinedly innocent eyes. *They must practice when I'm not around,* she thought. *On company time.*

"Wrong," she said softly. "You're wrong. As far as you're concerned, tomorrow isn't Christmas. Tomorrow is simply eight days until Demo date. Unless, of course, the product is ready to demonstrate now. In which case, you may all take tomorrow off. *Is* it ready to demonstrate now?"

"There's some real problems with it, Ms. Banks," one of the braver among the team of managers began slowly and carefully, as if explaining to a child. Banks drummed her nails on the desk. Just because she knew nothing about programming or the mysteries that went into producing a product didn't mean she was stupid. These people didn't need to think they could slip anything past her. "On the one hand it's supposed to be able to be accessed by government surveillance nets, on the other it's supposed to appeal to the consumer and be able to be the one place they can basically park their life for further access . . . there's a lot of security inconsistencies."

"That's concept," she said. "The concept is developed. Your job is to make it work."

A black woman somewhat senior of the others cleared her throat and said, "That's the real problem, Ms. Banks. This thing won't run. It's a non-starter. Haven't you seen our memos?"

"Of course I have. But surely it's nothing a team of geniuses such as yourselves can't fix? You and those hundreds of people on my payroll you said it would take to actually make it work—by the way, why weren't they put on twenty-four hour status also? The other buildings are dark . . ."

"They've *been* on twenty-four hour status, Ms. Banks," said a young Asian man. "And so have we and so have you. And it still won't run. So we"—he looked around the room—"we told everybody to go home for the holidays while we let you know that we're going to have to rethink this one completely—"

"What you are going to do is call all of those people back!" She spat the words one by one. "And work, as you were hired to do! This product is sold. If we don't have it ready by demo date on New Year's Day, this company stands to lose a major contract as well as congressional supporters of our status in the industry. *And* we will no doubt be sued by the government. I can tell you with considerable authority that tangling with the United States of America is no laughing matter."

"Of course not, Ms. Banks," a pretty blond said. "But that doesn't make our program run and we can't call all those people back because most of them left town and the roads are supposed to be getting worse all day and the airports are socked in already. By the time we got the teams reassembled, it would be too late to finish by New Year's Day anyway."

"Besides," a red-headed man said, "it wouldn't matter if every geek in the country was working on this turkey, it still wouldn't fly."

"Oh, no? Nevertheless, Databanks has a contract for one flying turkey and you have a contract to make sure that it flies. Therefore, as management staff, you will devote yourselves every hour of every day between now and the time your task is completed to accomplishing it. If you do, it had better be ready for that Demo in some form or another. If not, I will be speaking to our attorneys about breach of contract suits. Clear? Good," she said and left without waiting for an answer.

David, the marketing manager, strode out behind her as if he knew what he was doing, but he had to run to catch her at the elevator. "Ms. Banks, our presentation is effectively finished and I was wondering, not that it matters to me, but my kid is supposed to get to come and visit me, and well, I haven't seen her since her mother and I split up and she's going to have her tonsils out over New Year's—"

"And who's going to pay the doctor bills if Daddy gets fired?" Monica said, turning on him like spicy food eaten at bedtime. "You're not finished until I say you're finished, and I want the whole team together. Do I make myself clear?"

"Yes, ma'am," he said.

"Whew," said Curtis Lu, the project coordinator, when Monica Banks left the room. "I bet she took lessons from boa constrictors on mouse-hypnotizing to learn to do that."

"Her management style makes Brother Doug's approach look almost laid-back," agreed Sheryl, the project development manager. "I wonder if they teach them that where she used to work at the IRS or if it's just sort of a gift—"

"Past life experience in the Third Reich is more like it," Curtis said.

"Careful, comrade, the valls haff ears," John Beardesley, a test manager, said.

"Good. They need something now that Her Majesty has taken down and sold all the artwork," Sheryl said. "I can't tell one building from another anymore. I used to be able to navigate from Building Eight back to my office by starting with the naked garbageman painting in the atrium, turning left at the beaded thingy that looks like moss, and going down the stairs just past the sculpture of the giant eggplant wearing a backpack for a hat."

"And now she's ripped down our 'toons," mourned Harald, who was a designer. "Why didn't we form a union when we had a chance?"

"Because we had stock options back when Doug was alive, and we all are now what all of our team members fondly believe to be filthy rich management," Curtis said. "Though we've just been demoted to 'toonless peons."

"And now we have to work for The Evil Empress Monica, building software to spy on users all over this great free land of ours for her Cruel Empire."

"Fortunately, it just won't run—just won't run—just won't run—" John said, jerking his head like a needle across a cracked vinyl record.

"Unfortunately, we have contracts and she hass vays of making us code," John said, still in movie-Nazi mode. "You haff relatiffs still vorking for IBM?"

"The woman is obviously paranoid," Sheryl said. "My analyst would have a nervous breakdown trying to sort through all *her* stuff."

"Maybe it's just her way of, like, mourning?" Melody suggested. Melody looked like a Barbie doll with glasses and talked like she had a blond brain, but her IQ was at least 180.

Everyone was quiet for a moment, considering the possibility, and then Curtis said what was on everybody's mind. "Nah. She just hates geeks. Back to the salt mines."

They retired to spend the rest of Christmas Eve in their bleak, cartoonless offices, trying to get a machine to do something they wished it wouldn't.

Two

~

Eight-year-old Tina Timmons sat in the darkened office while her grandfather ran the carpet cleaner in the hallway. She wasn't just quiet as a mouse, she was a whole lot quieter. Mice were pretty noisy, really. She knew a *lot* about mice. Woke up with them on her sometimes. She had to be quieter than those scampery little monsters because if she wasn't, Grandpa would lose his job and then none of them would have enough to eat and she'd never get the operation her Uncle Jamie said would make her The Bionic Kid.

So she was quiet for that reason, but she was also usually pretty quiet, for though she looked fine from the waist up, she had what Grandpa called a "few little problems." Her good parts were her curly red hair, that everyone always said was so pretty, and her sort of weak but very inquisitive brown eyes that couldn't see very far but loved to read anything she could find from library books to shampoo bottle labels. Her arms were strong from working extra hard to help her legs, which had come rotated inward at the hip, knee, and ankle when she was born. And her fingers could draw and cut out her own paperdolls, make origami paper boxes, pandas, cranes, robots, dragons, and anything else she could find the scrap paper for. If her legs had been the only problem, she could have been left home, but she also had a faulty heart valve, so her heart didn't pump enough oxygen to her lungs for her to be able to catch her breath if she moved too fast. Because of her heart, Grandpa had to bring her to work now. Kids couldn't go to Mama's work at all, and Mama's younger brother and sister, Uncle Jamie and Aunt Brianna were only thirteen and twelve themselves; too little to take care of her if she had a heart attack. When she was little, Grandma had been there to help them, but then Grandma went away. Maybe, Tina suspected, the same place her own daddy had gone, but she didn't know. Grownups didn't talk about that stuff where she could hear.

Anyway, she wasn't any trouble to her grandpa because she was good at keeping still most of the time, unless she fell or bumped against something accidentally.

But she was especially quiet tonight because as of midnight, when they came to work, it was Christmas Eve morning and she was waiting and wondering what was going to happen next.

She wasn't waiting for or wondering about her Christmas present. She wanted a kitty but she knew the apartments didn't allow cats or dogs or ponies—only rats, mice, and cockroaches. There might be a little something, a candy bar maybe, in the sock she'd left hanging from the windowsill with those of her aunt and uncle. That was if Mama had scored a big tip from one of the customers and the mice didn't get to the candy bars first.

No, she was excited because she was waiting for her invisible friend to come back and help her put the final touches on the project she'd been helping him with. Christmas Eve was the time the two of them had been working toward since Halloween night, when he'd first appeared to her. Tonight, she and Grandpa would be staying home instead of working their midnight to eight A.M. shift because at midnight tonight, when Grandpa was usually getting out the vacuum and the dust rags, it would be the start of Christmas. If her friend was right and she had done everything correctly, something awesome was going to happen. It was all pretty mysterious and complicated, and she wished she could be there to see it happen, but her friend had said she'd know when it did, whether she was there or not.

Back in October, when Mama got her night job and Tina started coming to work with Grandpa, she'd thought it'd be pretty boring. Her being here had to be a secret, so Grandpa had made her a little nest under a desk with a sleeping bag and a throw pillow. It was one of those double desks, with half you keep a computer on and half you keep books and stuff on. She was supposed to sleep under the books part. There were still lots of books on the desk with titles that didn't make any sense. Grandpa had to move around the building doing the cleaning, but Tina was supposed to stay in her little nest and not make a peep so she wouldn't be found and Grandpa wouldn't get caught. She didn't know who the desk belonged to.

She had been lying there on Halloween night, looking up at the computer while outside Grandpa went from office to office, vacuuming, emptying trash baskets, cleaning glass. She had been wishing she had someone to talk to. She wasn't feeling very sleepy and she was lonesome. She was lonesome a lot. Mama and Grandpa had to sleep during the day, so she had to be quiet then, too. Uncle Jamie and Aunt Brianna were in school most of the time or playing with their friends someplace else or doing homework while "watching" her. Their school didn't have the money to take care of crippled kids like Tina, Mama said. Mama and Grandpa had to home-school her. Grandpa said it was that Senator Johansen who had taken away the school money for crippled kids, but Tina didn't know him. She didn't know much of anybody outside of her family.

But she knew from what all of them said that you could meet lots of people on computers. Talk to people all over the world. She struggled to her feet and stood by the keyboard. She was just really sort of running her hand over the keys, thinking about all those people, when her finger had accidentally pressed the power button.

Well, it made a beep and a clicking sound, and then all at once there was something that sounded like church music and words at the top read, "Program Manager."

"Here's your miracle, Banks. Make this good. You're on."

"I won't let you down this time." Then, "Hi. Who's there?"

"Tina," she typed, one letter at a time.

"You'll have to input faster than that, Tina. We've got a lot of work to do."

"I'm only 8," she protested.

"8? Perfect. I wasn't programming when I was 8 yet because the stuff wasn't available, but I would be, if I were 8 now. Now then, what you and I have to do is design a little game. You like games, Tina?"

"Yes," she typed cautiously. "What game is it? I don't have to do anything dumb if I lose, do I?"

There was a long wait at the other end. Then the typed words: "It's not that kind of a game. It's one we're making up. It's a secret. The winner—I hope—will be somebody the game helps if we play it right."

"Okay. How do we play?"

"We make it up. I'll show you how, only—look, it's a good thing you're a kid. That Program Manager is really sharp to have partnered me with you. When I was a kid, I never read story books. I always liked instruction books. Can you tell me who we should get to help somebody become a better person?"

"Umm—Mama likes Dr. Ruth."

"No, it's not that kind of change."

"Oprah?"

"It'd be better if it wasn't somebody who's still . . . around."

"I know! Scrooge!"

"No. No Ducks."

"Not Scrooge McDuck! That's different. I mean the Scrooge from the story. You know, the one who went from saying 'Bah! Humbug!' on Christmas Eve to 'Merry Christmas' the next morning."

"You're a very smart kid. Scrooge it is. We'll use old Scrooge. Okay with you?"

Tina started to answer when the Program Manager button, which had been dark, suddenly started glowing red and all of a sudden a symbol came on the screen that looked to Tina like the Star Trek Tricorder that Brianna got out of a cereal box a couple of weeks ago. Across the tricorder, words wrote themselves in fancy golden letters: "Make it so."

They had been working on the project for a while when Tina, weary of the words and symbols she didn't understand in spite of the computer guy's even less understandable explanations asked, "Where are you? Do you work here?"

"I used to own the place. I guess you might say I'm on sabbatical now. Only permanently."

Once he told her he used to own all the buildings and computers and was the boss, she figured it was okay to be on the computer as long as he was with her. She couldn't do much standing up, so she stacked books on the seat so she could reach the keyboard sitting, and piled books up to support her feet, and continued the conversation.

The computer guy wasn't always friendly and nice. He got mad when she couldn't keep up with him, but when she was gone, on Grandpa's days off, he really seemed to miss her, and when she came back, he was much nicer and more patient and explained more things. He told her that what they were doing was a kind of present, and who it was for, and about when he had been a little boy. He even answered some of her questions without making her feel dumb.

After a while, the two of them got to be real friends.

Every night that she came to work with Grandpa, her new friend would have lots of work for them to do together. So much that she began sleeping days, too, and she wasn't as lonesome anymore.

The night before Christmas Eve, they worked all night. She recognized some words, but they weren't in any kind of sensible order. Her friend told her, when she asked, that they were in something called *code*, which was what computer programs were written in.

"Is that what this is?" she asked. "A program?"

"Not exactly. It's sort of an override."

"Why?"

"Because it's the most important thing that will ever play on any of these machines."

"Wow! What is it, really?"

"Tina, do you know what a medium is?"

"You mean like a person who sees ghosts, not like what comes between small and large?"

"Right, but the person doesn't see the ghost, the ghost comes through the person. Well, this program we built is a little like that."

"Sounds kind of scary," she answered, and she was glad, as she sat alone in the dark room with just her friend's letters glowing green on the screen, that the sound of Grandpa's vacuum cleaner was coming from the next office.

"Don't be silly, Tina. The ghosts the Program Manager sends are to help people, not to scare them."

"Help them? Is the Program Manager like . . . are these ghosts really angels?" Wouldn't that be a great Christmas to have made an angel on one of the computers! Maybe it would unfurl its big, white, floaty, feathery wings right there on the screen and fly out and hand her a kitty and fix her heart and legs while it was at it. *I don't think so*, she said to herself, but her friend was typing back.

"Not exactly, not all of them, not yet anyway, but—you ask too many questions. Back to work."

They wrote lots more stuff she didn't understand except in little bits.

"There," her friend said. "Now nothing else can play while this is running. We've set it up with the past, present, future segments and customized buttons. We're ready to run it. Excited?"

"Yeah."

"Okay, then, type the password and let it run!"

"I've got to go home soon and I won't be back tomorrow because it's Christmas and Grandpa doesn't come to work. I gotta turn off the computer so Grandpa's boss won't think I was here."

"Doesn't matter. Once it starts, it will run on all the other computers. Go!"

She took a deep, rattling breath and typed, "Humbug." Christmas music began to play and pictures flickered by on the screen too fast for her to tell what they were.

Then, out in the hall, Grandpa started singing "Grandma Got Run Over by a Reindeer" which was their signal for her to hide. She hated to turn that computer off worse than she could remember hating anything, but she did, and then she curled up under the desk. "I forgot!" she said, as the footsteps outside approached and a woman began speaking to her Grandpa. "Merry Christmas!" she whispered to the empty monitor.

Maybe she just imagined it, but for the blink of an eye the screen seemed to come to life again and a man's sad, worried face looked down at her and gave her the smallest of smiles as he said, "Merry Christmas to you, too, Tina."

Three

⚭

Monica Banks stalked back through the barren halls to her office. Her mood was not improved by getting lost several times. She knew at once that she was lost in one section because she passed the lobby with the new spot of carpet showing against the old where a sculpture had been removed. Bright rectangles on the walls marked the former presence of paintings as well. Perhaps she really ought to invest in having the carpet taken up and tile put down so strips of fluorescent tape could mark particular areas, as they did in hospitals. Either that or more signs. She was glad she had failed to have the lights turned off in the unused sections over the holidays. Though it was after dawn outside, the weather was bad and these interior halls were gloomy. She kept expecting something to jump out at her—a crazed chainsaw-wielding killer, perhaps. Miles of long hallways with nothing but the sound of her own footsteps, which got quicker and quicker and quicker so that she was practically running when she heard the sound of a vacuum cleaner and voices.

Turning a corner, she beheld the cleaning man. Ah, then,

she was getting an early start. The cleaning staff left at eight A.M., and she'd already prodded her sluggish employees to get on with their job.

The man shut off his vacuum and bent to wind the cord around the handle, then looked up and saw her. She had the distinct impression that he turned to one of the side offices and said something she was still too far away to hear.

As she approached, he secured the cord, rose, and nodded. "Merry Christmas, Ms. Banks."

"Good morning," she said curtly, annoyed to be given personal holiday greetings by cleaning staff. She couldn't remember the man's name though she had been introduced to him by someone who said he'd been working there since the company moved to these quarters. "Who were you talking to?"

"No one, Ms. Banks. I was just singing," he said. "Christmas carols, like. Practicin' to go caroling tonight. 'Grandma got run over by a reindeer . . .'"

"I get the picture," she said, looking through the darkened glass panel into the office beyond. Books were stacked on the chair and the floor beneath it, presumably by the employee who, having finished his or her project, was now off someplace being maudlin about Christmas. The monitor screen was empty and dark, but she couldn't escape the feeling that the console would be warm if she touched it. She had the prickly feeling it had just been turned off. But she also definitely didn't feel like checking the office right at that moment, in this dark hallway with this low-level employee singing homicidal carols. So she simply told the man,

"No one's to mess with this equipment. It's extremely valuable, as I'm sure you'd know if its price was deducted from your paycheck. Only qualified staff are to handle it."

"Oh, yes, ma'am, Ms. Banks. I know that for sure. I don't ever touch it."

She hadn't actually caught him at it, so all she could say was, "Well, good. See that you don't. And sing on your own time." She stood there a moment more, debating about which turn to take.

"Is there anything else, Ms. Banks?"

"You, er, wouldn't know the way back to my office from here, would you?"

"Sure I would. Down the next hall, turn left, turn right, and there's the elevator. It'll let you out right in front of your place. You get lost, too?"

"Of course not. I was just making sure you knew."

"That's all right then," he said, and turned the vacuum cleaner back on as she left him, no longer singing, behind her.

Four

～

Later, at her own office computer, Monica tried to decide if she liked the title marketing had come up with for the new product. "Get a Life" sounded like a TV talk show to her.

Suddenly, the door to her private office swept open with a gust of air that smelled like pine needles on snow, as if the outdoors could filter through the many halls and doors between it and her. Bells jingled, and then someone large, wet, and cold enveloped her in an embrace and kissed her soundly on the top of the head and said, "Merry Christmas, Money!"

She swung around to face her attacker. "Wayne Reilly, don't you ever call me that, dammit! My name is Monica, as you very well know. I'd like to sue whoever thought that up!"

Wayne Reilly grinned back at her. He had been Doug's best buddy all through school and raided her meagre refrigerator all the time he was growing up. He still looked like a kid to her—okay, an aging kid. He must be at least forty now, but he had remained round-faced, jug-eared, and freckled, like the kid on the cover of Mad magazine, the "What Me Worry?" one. He failed to look contrite as his wet mittened hand proffered a wreath sprigged with mistletoe and holly. "Ho ho ho?" he said. "Relax, enjoy the holidays. You can't fight the press any more than you can fight death and taxes—" She glared at him.

"Ooops, sorry. Am I getting too personal again? Just say so."

"You're getting too personal again, Wayne."

"Don't be shy. I mean, I hate it when you hold stuff back. It's so bad for you . . ."

"Get out, Wayne. I've got work to do. How did you get past Brenda, anyway?"

"I bribed her with some marshmallow Santas."

"You've got a company of your own. Go run it."

"I've got a better boss than you do. He gives me days off, including all national holidays."

"I have a product that needs to be ready for demo by New Year's."

"Who doesn't? Besides, what I hear is you don't have a product yet."

"You've been spying on us!"

He shrugged. "Word gets around."

"Does word also say it's an extremely important government contract, and I'm working on the project right now, which is classified, thank you, so you shouldn't have even come in?"

"Nope, word says, actually, that it's one of those things maybe it would be better if it didn't get built . . ."

"Are you suggesting sabotage?"

"I'm suggesting ethics. This system you're producing isn't just another address book program. You're building something that will potentially allow a serious invasion of people's privacy."

Her smile was humorless. "I'm quite used to that. Listen, Wayne, you and Doug may have been lucky enough to make big money following your bliss or whatever with these machines, but you and I both know that Doug knew nothing about business. He has left the company with some outstanding debts here."

There was anger and scorn in her voice and Wayne said gently, "Monica, it's not like he took the money and runna Venezuela, if you'll pardon a Belefonteism. He died. He left his shares and his position and his life's work to you."

"Of course he did," she said. "Who else would he leave it to? You? He already bought you out, and you've received all you're going to from Databanks. He knew I had the good business sense to put this outfit back on its feet and bail it out of trouble with Uncle and that's exactly what I intend to do."

"You talk like it's an overextended mortgage or a credit card debt. This is a multibillion-dollar concern."

"The principles are the same. Simply on a grander scale. Now, if you'll excuse me, I've got work to do."

"What I meant was," Wayne continued, patronizingly, no less, this kid who used to cost her a small fortune in Diet Pepsis and Cheetos, "Doug worked night and day and all holidays to build this place until he dropped dead over his keyboard. Not recommended. You gotta take time off some-times. Come on, Monica. Tomorrow is Christmas. I'm cook-ing. It's supposed to snow. Santa Claus is coming to town. Whaddaya say?"

"I already said it," she said, rising, pulling him out of his chair and propelling him toward the door. "Go away. I'm busy. Mind your own business, and I'll mind mine."

Nerd! she thought angrily. *No social skills whatsoever. Just like Doug. Just like all of these weird people working here.*

As she showed Wayne out, Brenda, shamefaced, said, "Senator Johansen is here to see you, Ms. Banks."

The tall, white-haired man with the expensive dental work carried an elaborately wrapped gift. To him, Monica was all smiles and graciousness. "Bob! How nice to see you!"

"Since I couldn't talk you into going to dinner with me last night, I had to come by and bring you a little holiday cheer."

They entered her office, the senator still talking as fast as a TV shopping channel show host.

"I did want to speak to you about getting your support for the bill I'm proposing. It would abolish unnnecessary sub-sidizing of housing and support money for unwed mothers and their offspring, which clearly does nothing but encour-age more dependency. Instead, the mothers would be re-quired to go to training and to work on state projects. The children would be less expensively housed and better cared for in a state boarding school facility where they can receive occupational training in the same useful trades their moth-ers are learning: cleaning, maintenance, cooking, etcetera.

Why, the state would even find them jobs where they could work off the cost of their living expenses and schooling."

"Sounds like a wonderful plan," Monica said. "These women could use some supervision till they learn to control themselves. And all those children, just growing up to make the streets unsafe while their mothers are off having more! I knew as a very young girl that I had to earn my own way in the world and I did the responsible thing and had no children for an employer to worry about or my fellow citizens to support with their tax money. I wonder why this generation of girls can't just use birth control or, better yet, simple restraint."

"So few women are as wise as you, Monica dear. Aren't you going to open your present?" the senator asked.

"Oh, you shouldn't have," she said quite sincerely since she didn't want to incur obligation she might not wish to repay. "I didn't get you anything." She hadn't, in fact, gotten anything for anyone. She never bought Christmas presents. Far too expensive. Nor cards. Why write once a year to people you didn't care enough about to write to the rest of the year? Besides, it was all a ploy to make the card companies rich. Better to keep the money in her own pocket.

"Nonsense, my dear. Your dear brother would have wanted me to look after you . . ."

"Oh, Bob, you've been a real knight in shining armor, defending Databanks to Congress and the courts. It's been so difficult since Doug died." She smiled up at him, her most gracious smile.

"Nonsense, my dear. What's good for Databanks is good

for America, and I'm the first to say so. Won't you open your present now?"

"Oh, a fruitcake. How—lovely," she said. Good. She no longer felt any obligation concerning the gift. She loathed fruitcake. Still, she had to pretend to be pleased. "If you don't mind, Senator—Bob—I'd like to share it with my staff. They're working so hard on finishing our project, I'm afraid many of them have had no opportunity to celebrate properly."

"Do as you wish, of course, my dear, though I had hoped you'd accept it as a *personal* token from me."

A personal fruitcake! If he thought a fruitcake was personal, then there was more than one fruitcake in the room. "Er—certainly," she said. Bob was perfectly correct, of course. There was no reason to throw the fruitcake as a sop to the whining of the employees about the free company cafeterias she'd closed. She had no need to help the employees, really. They got paid, didn't they?

"After the project is over, Monica, I'd really like to have you over to dinner to celebrate. I have a lovely houseboat on Lake Union."

He also had a wife, three children, an ex-wife, and a mistress, according to the press, but none of *them* controlled an international corporation.

"It sounds divine, Bob. I'll look forward to it as a special treat."

He looked deeply and meaningfully into her eyes while kissing her hand. "The first of many, I hope. Merry Christmas."

"Same to you," she said, walking him to the door.

"Ms. Banks?" Brenda stopped her from reentering the office. "Ms. Banks, what about those contribution requests from the Salvation Army, the March of Dimes, Paralyzed Veterans, the Gospel Mission for the Homeless, UNICEF, and United Way this year? You said you'd review them."

"I have," she said, impatient at all the interruptions. Returning to her desk, she picked up the senator's Christmas gift and handed it to Brenda. "Here. Let them eat fruitcake."

Five

⌘

By evening, the rain outside had turned to sleet and Monica thought her employees should be glad she had required them to remain at work instead of having to commute on the icy highways.

Doug had, of course, left her the mansion he had built for himself, but it was full of complex electronic controls and she preferred the suite of rooms adjoining the office. They were simpler and more conventionally appointed, though still furnished with computers in every room, including the bath.

She decided she might as well fix herself something to eat. From her window, she saw a pizza delivery van pull up outside the building, and the delivery man emerged with a pile of boxes. After a few minutes, one of the employees met him at the door and took custody of the boxes. She had forbidden any deliveries inside the building. Her competitors were perfectly capable of disguising themselves to steal Databanks's secrets.

Well, she had a TV dinner left in the fridge, she thought. Last one, and she was tired of them. But if the cat went away, the mice would play, so she had to stay within pouncing range. Honestly, these were supposed to be such intelligent people. Why couldn't they just act like adults and get on with the job? She knew they weren't applying themselves. They'd always come through on deadlines for Doug.

While the dinner was in the microwave, she clicked on the news.

KING-5 showed a huge traffic snarl on I-5. A reporter who looked as if she was trying not to freeze to death stood, microphone in gloved hand, near the freeway entrance. Snowflakes coming down big as teacups and thick as excuses at a tax audit fell around her at a strong slant, propelled by the heavy north winds the weatherman had mentioned.

The Dow Jones was down, the Sonics had lost again, some stupid people had managed to burn down an apartment building including a set of parents and a small child. Four children survived out of the same family. *Probably they'd be taking up beds in Bob Johansen's boarding school when it opened*, she thought sourly. *Might be a better neighborhood for them.* She was about to change the station, hating the way the camera dwelled on the children's sad little faces while the anchor maundered on about homeless orphans at Christmastime, when the image disappeared in a crackling blizzard of electronic snow.

"Damn," Monica said, fearing electrical problems that might slow down her little elves slaving away in their offices.

She checked her computer screen and it was also filled with snow. "Double damn," she said. But as she started to turn away, the snow squiggled about like the iron filings on a magnetic drawing toy she had bought for Doug when he was a child. He hadn't liked it. Said the magnetism was bad for his project.

But like the iron filings, the black-and-white distortion suddenly took on a recognizable form—black eyes burning a hole in an oval—a face, of white, white snow—mouth, chin, ears—Wait a minute. She knew those ears. And the nose—that nose! The face was Doug's. She turned around to the television. The image on the TV screen was identical to the one on the computer. How could that be? Was the television perhaps transmitting an old image of Doug and doing a follow-up story on his death—yet another story where they'd refer to her as "Former IRS tax auditor, heiress Monica 'Money' Banks"? But how could the computer be picking up the same image? Was one of her loyal employees screwing around with her equipment?

She had never seen this shot of Doug before. This looked like his face the day he died, after he died, except the eyes were open.

Then the mouth opened as well. "Hi, Sis," it said.

"If this is some kind of a computer trick or a video splice, it's childish and mean," she said, not expecting an answer.

"It's not, Sis, and there's nothing up my sleeves, either. In fact," he raised arms into the screen, arms that had rotted away in places, despite that expensive coffin, to bone. "No sleeves."

"This is a truly tasteless joke, whoever you are. My

brother may have just been a millionaire to you, but he was—"

"Your brother. God, Moni, you can be so dense. It's me, Doug. I came to warn you, okay?"

"*You're* warning *me?* That's impossible. You're—I mean, Doug is—dead."

"Well, yeah, I know. But don't get hung up on details. This was originally scheduled to just be a phone call from the dead, but I said, hey, you know what? Me, Doug Banks, the techie millionaire, making a simple *phone* call, well, it's not only dated, it's completely out of character. So I was allowed to tinker with the production values and we've arranged to bring in someone I think . . . I'm getting carried away here. . . ."

Monica smiled, not warmly. "You always did."

"But I'm not the only one, Moni. There's got to be some changes made, Sis. Before it's too late."

"I know it's getting late, and those idiots you hired still haven't come up with a product," she said. "But they do understand that they are not leaving here until they do or I'll sue their genius asses off. Say, as long as you're doing some computer haunting, how about haunting *them* and maybe giving them some otherworldly tips on how to finish this product before Databanks goes broke?"

A low moan from the computer rose to a wailing cry that completely filled the room until she had to hold her hands over her ears to make it stop. At last, when she couldn't stand any more of it, the wailing stopped.

"Oh, Ssissss," hissed the image of her brother's face, albeit in black-and-white. You'd think such a technical genius could have managed color, but then, knowing him and the way he thought old-time movies were so cool, he might have done it on purpose. It was beginning to break up, to dissolve into snow, which was what was making it hiss, she thought. "You're misssssing the point . . . point . . . point." The hiss was now accompanied by an echo and a blurring of Doug's snowy features.

"Doug! Don't you dare just leave me like this! You have some explaining to do!"

She touched the keyboard, thinking there must be some command that could clarify her brother's image and speech, but her fingers were still inches from the keys when a jolt of static electricity knocked her backward. It was then that she noticed that the whole room was filled with static snow, just like the computer screen, and while her clothing clung to her in pools and ripples and her nylons crackled, the hairs on her skin and head stood straight up, tingling and quivering with the charge.

"Moni, I haven't got long," the image said, resolving again. "And neither have you. You need to pay attention. We've both always needed to pay attention. I am not a dream. I am not a problem with your monitor. I am not a problem with your reception. Please do not attempt to adjust your terminal again. I am a ghost, Sis." At least he had stopped hissing.

"The ghost in the machine, I presume?" she asked tartly.

He asked, a little annoyed at her denseness, which had been his usual tone when he was alive, "Where *else* would

I haunt? Where else did I ever spend any time? I spent all my life turning my back on the world looking into computers and now it looks like I'm doomed to spend my afterlife inside a computer looking out at what I missed. Only problem is, of course, most places the computer doesn't offer much of a vantage point for all the things I'm supposed to have done, like enjoying Christmas and cherishing my loved ones."

"Cherishing your loved ones? Give me a break! You never cared about anything except your project of the moment while you were alive, and you seemed perfectly happy. Why should you regret that, now that you're dead, for heaven's sakes? Do they make you go through therapy when you die?"

"No, but you're stuck for all eternity with the choices you made in life. This is not just a phase I'm going through, being inside a computer. Except for this one time, I am doomed to haunt terminals. I give a whole new meaning to the term *vaporware*. I ride the ethernet forever, the—er—man who never returned." A deep sigh came through the computer like a gust of wind that rattled the vertical window blinds and blew Monica's hair straight back.

"Well, yes, fine, but why bring it up now? I have work to do, you know."

"Because it's Christmas, and you shouldn't *be* working. You should be . . . um . . . rejoicing?"

"Oh, really? And what's what I do with Christmas got to do with you being dead and fouling up the business you left me by haunting valuable memory space?"

"Because, sister *dearest*, Christmas has always been about

second chances. And I'm here to give you yours, which will maybe give me mine. So I hope you'll pay attention and not blow it."

"What do you mean second chances?"

"Did you think the kid in the manger was thought up by the heavenly merchandising department just to create a boom market in creches and Chinese-made tinsel stars and treetop angels that say at programmable intervals, "Unto us a child is born!" I think not. I've learned a thing or two since I've been dead, and let me tell you, it's come as a shock to me. The deal is, that kid came to give the world a second chance, take it or leave it. Use it or lose it. No pain no gain. And it's not just a churchy thing, Sis. It's about looking out for each other and paying attention to other people for reasons other than to see what they'll buy. I . . . uh . . . didn't get that for some reason."

"But you were gifted! The gifted have an obligation to develop their gifts!"

"Oh, yeah, but it's how you use them that counts. You're supposed to give a little as well as take—"

"Now you really don't sound like yourself. Are you sure you haven't been hanging around with a lot of liberal, New Age people since you died?"

"None of that stuff matters. Nobody asks if the group you hung out with was cool or not, just who were you, where you were when you were needed, and what did you do. Rank doesn't have any privilege here. I always had to make things work *my* way when I was alive. I only interfaced with people when I was in charge, when I was running things. And now

I can't run anything, except just this one last time, my first Christmas away from home, as it were, my second chance to help you change."

"This is way creepy, Douglas. I don't want to change . . . and I don't understand why you're behaving this way or why you're preaching at *me* for heaven's sake, or why you're in black-and-white and talking in that hollow B-grade horror movie voice."

"It's a ghost thing, okay? Let's just say the Unitarians do not have all the answers. Moni, Sis, listen to me before you've wasted your entire life trying to stay safe by scaring everyone else to pieces. Before you waste it keeping score and making sure you always have as much as the next guy— as you think I did. I hate to tell you this, Moni, but I had zip and you currently have zip and there is an awful lot to be had that you're not even going for."

"Now you sound like that silly purple dinosaur."

"Maybe so, but you're the one in danger of becoming extinct. Look, it's Christmas. Did we ever once have Christmas together after I left home?"

"We didn't have time."

"Bull! You're my only sister, my last living relative. You raised me, and yet we never really were together. I was building my launchpad for cyberspace and you were gouging taxes out of terrified people."

"My job supported your precious research, mister, and don't you dare think being dead is any excuse for criticizing me!"

But the ghost's wail rose above her until she swallowed the rest of what she would have said.

"I'm not. I can't criticize anyone. I chewed up employees and spit them out. Because it was tax deductible, and convenient, I built a fancy work environment no one looked at because they all had their heads as far up their derrieres as I had. I gave to charity because it was deductible, too, and when it wasn't anymore, I stopped giving. All the giving I ever did was because of some tax break I'd get!"

"Then I wish you'd given more, too," Monica sniffed, "because you've left this business in quite a financial snarl."

The ghost heaved a deep, sad sigh, like a wind trying to blow through the boughs of ancient forest and finding only stumps.

Doug's face, however, was the same dead-still mask of static snow and blackness as he said, mumbling as he used to when trying to understand some arcane bit of programming, "So what? You're a couple mil short of enough to make the next multimillion-dollar deal? I used to think I was in deep financial doo doo when that happened, too, and I never thought how many people my petty cash would feed, how I could have put all the brainpower here to work trying to figure out how to make up for too much war, too much destruction, too little clean water, too few trees, too little food. . . ." Though the face didn't change expression, she suddenly knew it was addressing her again, and the volume rose again. "I only thought about the next cool tech thing to do and how much money it would make for me so I could build the next cool thing."

"You were a very busy man, and besides, there's government agencies to see to that—"

At this, the screen broke up again and the electricity popped all around her for a frighteningly long time before Doug's ghost re-formed and he said, "More BS. The phrase 'Life is not a dress rehearsal' is not just a bumper sticker, Sister dear. I had to go through a lot to arrange this. I've been here in this machine watching you screw things up, screw your life up, ever since I died, but now is the only time you'll ever see me. I can't stay and argue with you. Why should I? We never listened to each other, anyway. But I did arrange for someone to come who's had a little experience at this kind of thing. Someone who's maybe a little more on your—pardon the expression—wavelength than I ever was. The spirit debuts at one, with encores at two and three. Be there and be afraid, Monica, be very afraid."

"Doug, Doug, I'm trying to get a product ready for Demo here. You understand that. Can't your friend just tell me what he wants the first time and get it over with? I'm afraid your appearance may be seriously screwing up the computers."

"Oooooooh, Monica, I knew you'd react that way. I knew you'd try to cop out and say, 'Oh, it was only a dream,' or something else lame like that. Hence the three-time thing, so even you can't possibly ignore it." The ghost moaned again, suddenly sending shocks popping throughout the static-filled room. "Heads up, Sis. It's now or later, and you're really not going to like later . . ."

And with that, the face broke up once more and the static snow swirled into a vortex, sucking in the snow from all over the room, causing the microwave to short out, the silverware to bounce on the table, and the trade magazines to fly around the room like ghosts themselves. Monica cowered away from it, huddling into a little ball on the sofa, the cushion held in front of her knees, until the room had more or less returned to normal.

Six

~~~

Monica awoke from her nap on the couch and looked around at the room. Every book was in place, the sports news on the television, and the icon for Get a Life was on the computer screen. "Stress," she said to herself, her dream still vivid. "I must be more stressed-out than I thought. After we finish this project, I'll fire all those geniuses and hire people loyal to me. Then it'll be better."

She sat down at the computer station again, albeit some-what edgily, but nothing crackled, no snow appeared on the high-resolution screen, and she thought maybe she'd have beginner's luck with this and crack the problem with some-thing simple that hadn't occured to her brilliant employees.

It would have to be something very simple. She had been trying to learn programming, but it made very little sense to her. Besides, though it was good to understand what it was your help did, she was sure, it seemed silly to have a metaphorical watchdog and bark herself.

The program just sat on the screen in front of her and burped at the same place every time, shortly after it was booted up. Usually the screen simply locked up and nothing would move without another hard boot.

This time, when she flipped the switch back on, the Get a Life icon appeared briefly but instead of burping was followed by a brief screen full of snow. The knuckles of one trembling hand were at her teeth while her other hand reached for the switch when suddenly the snow was replaced with a clear, full-color, almost three-dimensional image of an elderly man in old-fashioned dress. He looked as if he were caught in the headlights of a truck.

Seven

❦

Ebenezer Scrooge, the word "humbug" still droning through his mind, opened his eyes. A face, young and grinning, flashed before him and disappeared. Suddenly he was looking all at once at dozens, hundreds, of other faces. At least as many as he would once have met near his own offices in London.

Who on earth could these people be, and why did he get the impression that, though they seemed to be a crowd, they each seemed unaware of the other and looked at him as if he were a personal discovery. They were such strange faces, not the sort one saw in London every day, young men and women, no old people or children. Some of the young men could have been clerks from their pale and studious demeanors, but they were shabbily dressed for the occasion in what appeared to be their underwear. More alarming, the young women were in a similar state of semidress, one bearing the legend across her bosom, "The Grateful Dead." So at least he was still among the deceased, it seemed.

There were an Asian face and two black faces as well.

Most puzzling to find a crowd in any part of London containing all of these people in the same situation.

At least he did not seem to be lying in a closed coffin, ready to scratch at the lid like a character from the pen of some demented, drug-crazed poet, he thought with relief. Still, it was quite disorienting.

Momentarily, he were able to focus on one particular female face, which was looking at him as if she were a judge and he were Jack the Ripper.

She was otherwise an ordinary enough lady, not yet old, though her expression belied that impression. Her face, though round-cheeked, bore hard, thick eyebrows over what might have been lovely blue eyes, had they not been narrowed with suspicion. Her rosebud of a mouth was held in a thin line. Lines of deep discontent ran from nose to chin and furrowed her otherwise creamy brow as well. She at least was decently though peculiarly clad in what appeared to be a gentleman's shirtwaist and waistcoat, though her gender was readily apparent in the shirtwaist's conformation. Her hair was unbecomingly short and worn close to her scalp, its rebellious tendency to curl seeming to give her horns. She might be the maiden daughter of some particularly bleak clergyman, from the look of her.

"Who are you supposed to be," she demanded in a growl at once dismissive and impatient, "Santa Claus?"

"Not at all, madam, although it's a flattering error. I am Ebenezer Scrooge, Esq. The late Ebenezer Scrooge, Esq. And whom, may I ask, have I the pleasure of addressing?"

"Tiny Tim, you idiot. *Not!*" she said, leaning toward him, an extremely unpleasant look slitting her eyes into chasms of glacial blue scorn. "You know very well who I am. I am Monica Banks. If you're the ghost my brother's ghost was talking about, funny he didn't mention me, don't you think? If you are a by-product of my own stress overload, then I invented you and you have to know who I am. If you are, as I suspect, an elaborate hoax, then I am your boss and I am not amused and would like to ask if you think you're such a hot dog that a New Year's deadline leaves you spare time for freelance work. Not to mention that you're in violation of your contract. That could be expensive for you. Do I make myself perfectly clear?"

And with that, she stabbed a finger toward Ebenezer and it was as if she had slammed a door in his face, for he no longer beheld her or the room in which she had been.

"Well!" Scrooge said to himself. "Monica Banks is certainly a rude young woman."

"And this is news?"

Scrooge was suddenly looking into the craterous pockmarks of a bespectacled young man. This one had the decency to wear a shirt open over his underwear. No necktie or cravat, no waistcoat or jacket. His eyes were distorted by the spectacles so that they appeared very large and almond brown. His black hair was cut into a bristle all over his head. This was the Asian gentleman. Scrooge had never actually exchanged words with anyone of that race.

"Good day to you, sir," he said.

The Asian gentleman, little more than a boy actually,

jumped up immediately and ran to the door of his room to call out, "Hey, you guys. That glitch we saw on the screen a few minutes ago! It's back, and it *talks*."

Scrooge took the opportunity to look about the room. It was a small and quite ordinary room. Well, perhaps not entirely ordinary. A window showed that although it was very gray outside, it was not yet dark. Raindrops splashed against the pane. He saw no fire, nor even a small grate to hold one. The interior was lit, quite brightly, not by candles or oil lamps, but by some sort of glowing glass orb that gave off light as steady and bright as sunshine. The door had glass around it and affixed to this glass were the tattered remnants of many small paneled drawings. Scrooge tried to examine them, and found he was prevented by a barrier of some sort that would not allow him to fully enter the room. Curious.

The young man returned, this time with many of the faces Scrooge had first seen, peering over his shoulders.

"Wow, look, it *is* back. Not on my screen yet, Curtis. What did you do to get it to come up again? Phenomenal full-screen video," a young woman with wild blond curls said.

"So what do you call it, man?" asked a fellow with a dark beard and hair slicked back into a horse's tail.

"I dunno, John. It just zapped into the middle of my coding. I hope I didn't lose everything I've done in the last twenty minutes."

"Well, see if you can get back to what you were working on." This suggestion came from a portly man the color of strong tea.

"What? Have you flipped, Phillip?" the Asian man addressed as Curtis asked. "Make it go away? This is interactive TV, man. Listen to him."

"A demo date is sacred. Haven't you been listening to Miz Money talking? Whatever this guy is, he ain't code. Shut him down," Phillip said.

"Killjoy. I don't get to have any fun. But okay. So, nice knowing you, dude. I'm escaping now. Bye," Curtis said, stabbing at a button.

But this time, Scrooge resolved not to be put off or have the door slammed in his face. "Here now, you," Scrooge said in the voice he'd used to strike terror into the hearts of tenants and clerks before his transformation. "I'm tired of this rudeness. You have a few questions to answer before I'm done with you!"

"Hey! I hit Alt-4 and nothing happened. That should have closed his program."

"Whoa!" John said, scratching his beard thoughtfully. "It won't let you out, huh? So much for today's work. Okay I can handle that. Do a hard boot and see what happens."

Curtis stabbed a finger again but Scrooge raised his cane and shook it at the fellow, adamant not to be ignored. Peculiar, that they should bury him with his cane. Convenient, however. "You there! Stop, I say!"

"He's . . . still . . . there," the curly-headed woman said. "I don't think we're in Windows anymore, Toto."

"Whatever are you talking about, madam? Of course I am still here, and I demand to know where I am, who you are, and just what is going on here."

"This is rich!" John cried, slapping his thighs and hooting in a voice entirely too loud for comfort.

"Who thought you up, gramps?" the blond asked as sweetly as she might ask a lost child what his mother looked like. "How do you work?"

"Could be one of the network guys messing with our heads," Curtis said doubtfully.

"I bet I know who he is, Melody," Phillip said. "I'll bet he's a present from Wayne—a new Wild Web toy to slow us down and make us wish we'd jumped ship with him. That's it, isn't it?" Phillip said, pointing a finger at Scrooge's nose in a most ill-mannered way. "You're from Wayne, aren't you?"

Scrooge started to give him his sternest glare, and then realized that perhaps, for all his rudeness, the man could be correct. "I'm afraid I don't know," Scrooge admitted. "How would one go about finding this Wayne?"

"I'll see if I can send you back to him right now," Curtis said, and he disappeared from in front of the screen for a moment. "Pulling the plug," he said to the others.

"He's still hee-eere," John told him. "Maybe someone is messing with your instrument. Let's take the lid off." They did so and poked around in the innards of a large roughly square beige metal box located next to Scrooge. Scrooge felt a few odd tinglings as they unplugged this and that, removed and replaced this and that, but nothing seriously affected him now that he realized he was in control of whether or not he stayed. Miss Banks's action had simply taken him by surprise.

"Nada," someone said finally, and they reassembled the box.

"Well, I'm going to see if I can get back into what I was working on," Curtis said and resumed tapping at the letters and numbers located just beneath Scrooge's chin.

Scrooge watched with some interest. The keys were very like the typewriting machine, which was just coming into use toward the end of his life. He had thought, the year he died, that he might purchase one for his office, to aid in the making up of bills and the printing of notices granting extensions to those unable to pay their rents for some reason or other. Formerly, he would never have spared the expense even to write the many eviction notices he had once sent out. The Christmas the ghosts had visited him had changed his business practices year round, however; so much so that although he had a slimmer profit margin at the end of his life, he had many more friends.

"It's locked up," Curtis said. "I tried to get out on the Net, too, but I can't lose this image long enough to reach Wild Web. I think we've got a major bug here, guys."

"Yeah," said Miriam, "and if this guy is really Ebenezer Scrooge, I guess we'd call him a *hum*bug, eh?"

"Most certainly not, young lady," Scrooge said to her. "I am a quite genuine manifestation, and I am currently in charge, so I'll thank you not to insult me."

"Be careful, Mir," John said. "He's right, and Melody's right. If this is really Ebenezer Scrooge, we've gone through the looking glass into the twilight zone and are now working with the Scrooge Operating System."

"Oh, no!" a light-brown young woman groaned. "I thought if I didn't watch TV and stayed away from high school plays, I'd avoid seeing another remake of *Christmas Carol*! Don't tell me someone's turned it into an operating system. This thing has to be a virus that *ate* the operating system. And a CD-ROM would have been bad enough."

"A virus that keeps on the screen even after the machine's been disconnected? I think not. I think we are privileged here to see the first signs of independent artificial intelligence. The Scrooge Operating System it is, or SOS, which seems an appropriate enough acronym when you think about it."

Scrooge did not quite understand the language these people were using. It seemed to be English, but so many of the words were in the wrong places. However, they seemed to understand him well enough when they weren't trying to disregard him or dismiss him altogether, so he ventured a question. "This Mrs. Banks: I take it from my brief interview with her that she is your employer?"

Curtis looked around, then answered the question quite civilly, having finally decided to treat Scrooge as another person. "For the time being," he said. "Some of us are only on contract, but some, like Sheryl," he nodded to the young woman whose color resembled strong tea with a great deal of milk, "have been here since Doug and Wayne founded Databanks."

"You wouldn't know it was the same place," Sheryl said with a woeful shake of her head. "Would you, Harald?" she asked another fellow, this one thin, dark, and bespectacled and perhaps a bit older than the others.

He shook his head sadly and held up a slice of pie with what appeared to be cheese melted on it. "Nope. Look at this. Cold pizza. On Christmas Eve, no less. Dragonlady closed all the cafeterias after five P.M. and charges more than a five-star restaurant to eat there, plus we get only a half hour."

Phillip chimed in, "When Doug was alive, they were always open and *free*, so if you were working on a problem at two A.M., you could still get a noshie."

"She brought in *time clocks*," Melody said with a delicate shudder.

"Sold the art collection, too," Sheryl added forlornly. "I could tell which building I was in by that art collection. Now all the interiors look the same. I was lost for three days once trying to get back from the rest room."

"Pay toilets," a red-haired woman interjected.

"I used to be able to tell where *I* was from Matt-in-development's inflatable shark hanging from his ceiling, Karen-the-coder's aquarium, tester Bob's stuffed gorilla, and the different *Doonesbury*, *Far Side*, and *Peanuts* cartoons on people's windows, but they're all gone now," Curtis said, shaking his head, grieving for what had gone before. "All gone."

Scrooge could tell they were very upset, but he hardly considered these complaints to be on a par with those of the folk he had found, once he took notice, to be starving, freezing, or perishing of disease and poverty in London during his own time. Still, he had come to realize in his latter years that working conditions were most important to employees.

"I read that she's closed off all but one bathroom, one bedroom, and a kitchen in Doug's mansion," the red-headed woman said. "She's letting the estate grow wild, like the grounds here."

"Not for long, Miriam," Curtis said. "She's going to sell Databanks's old-growth forest to Beaver Construction and let them subdivide the campus grounds for condos."

In the fervor of their complaints, they seemed to have forgotten entirely that they had not believed Scrooge to be real. Not that he was sure he was. But their comments served to reaffirm his suspicion of why he was where he was, wherever that was, which he did not know. Nor did he know when it was, for he felt that these people belonged to a quite different time, such as Mr. Jules Verne might have speculated upon in his stories. Before the Christmas with the ghosts, Scrooge would have disbelieved this perception, himself, or found it unsettling. But he had found that traveling through time could be instructive for him, and he was certain, now, that his current travels were intended to be instructive for others. Whenever this was, he knew one important thing. No matter which year this was, it was Christmastime, and Christmas was being ignored.

"Never you fear," he told them, feeling full of resolve. "I am here to see that you have a merry Christmas, after all."

"Merry Christmas?" Sheryl asked. "Who has time for Christmas? We've got work to do."

"Yeah, who has time for all that card and candles and jingle bell stuff?" Phillip agreed.

"It's just another cheap commercial excuse to make a buck," John added. "Not, mind you, that I don't like bucks."

"I always get very depressed around Christmas, personally," Harald said.

"I might get into Kwanzaa, but I'm usually just finishing up a big project and try to go to Tahiti instead," Sheryl said.

"Well, I'm Buddhist, but my family still has a big gathering with a tree, and I wish I was there instead of freezing my butt off here, half starving, and talking to a computer screen," Curtis said. He snapped his fingers suddenly. "Hey, I've got it! Maybe this is an interactive phone call that's been patched in here—"

"Curtis, we turned off the system and looked under the hood," Phillip told him. "If someone had cross-wired a video phone, we'd know about it by now. We have here an unexplained communications system using a seasonal avatar to give us a Christmas freakout. Maybe it's Wayne, after all, but if so, he's onto something we haven't even thought about yet."

"So, come on, gramps, give. Who are you really?" Sheryl asked.

"I told you, I'm Ebenezer Scrooge. In person—well, in a manner of speaking. I used to manage properties in London, you see, and was very good at it, except that I—"

"We know who Ebenezer Scrooge is," she said impatiently. "What we want to know is, who's behind that wrinkly mask. Cause whoever it is, he or she is jamming our system when we've got work to do."

"I assure you, my dear young lady, there is no one behind me."

"Something's going on above him, though. Oh! Look! It's an icon that says "Program Manager" like on the early Windows Op Systems. But I've never seen one shaped like a tricorder and all gold and glowy in Gonzo-gothic script like that!" John said.

And abruptly the room and all its inhabitants melted away like snowflakes.

Eight

⟨⟩

Monica Banks did not look pleased to see Scrooge again, but he hadn't supposed she would. So when she reached for the button this time, he was prepared. He knew she could not shut him out if he did not wish it.

"Now, now, my dear girl, that simply will not do," he said waggling his finger at her when she tried it, without so much as a "How do you do" or a "Merry Christmas." "You don't really want me to go, my dear. You see, I begin to understand my purpose here now, and it's very much in your best interests that I be here."

"Do tell," she said. "And what might that be, pray? Other than to hold up production and bankrupt my company, that is. And don't call me 'girl' or 'dear.' I won't be patronized in my own company."

"No, indeed," Scrooge said. "I should say not. Perish the thought. Well then, esteemed madam, if it pleases you or if it does not, I am here for your benefit."

"You bring a ghostly piece of programming that will make

my project run?" she asked. "Because that's all I want out of anybody."

"That seems very little to ask, whatever it is," he said. "But first, let me say that now I do quite understand your discomfiture at my presence. Something quite similar happened to me once, and it was very upsetting. Very. But instructive. You see, Miss Banks, I believe I am either to announce the visit of three ghosts—"

"Been there, done that!" she snapped. "I already had a dream where my brother's ghost was announcing the visit of . . . ohmigod." The snappiness drained out of her and she slumped in her chair. "Another ghost."

"Very well. That narrows the field considerably. Then I must be the ghost of Christmas Past."

"Wait a minute. He said you'd be coming three times."

"Will I now? How odd. I received visitations from three specters, myself—four altogether, if you count Marley, and since counting was Marley's life, I believe one must indeed count Marley."

"Doug's ghost didn't tell you?" she asked. "I mean, didn't he send you here?"

"I'm as puzzled about how I came to be here as you yourself seem to be, my—Miss Banks, but I believe we have sorted it out. Very well—ahem—" He cleared his throat and attempted to sound properly somber and spectrally authoritative. "I am the Ghost of Christmas Past. Follow me."

"What if you're all there is?"

"I beg your pardon?"

"You got four. You said so. It says so in every stupid Christmas play and TV takeoff you see. Three ghosts, plus the prequel. Christmases Past, Present, and Future, and Marley. So how come I only get you and Doug? Downsizing?"

"I'm not sure. Since I didn't know of your brother's visit, it is unlikely I would know about other specters that are to appear to you."

"This gets more reassuring all the time. You know what I think? I think you're another bad dream. I'm so tired and stressed-out, I've fallen asleep again, and you're my follow-up nightmare. A little something to waste my time when I have a job to do. Either that or you, Doug, the whole thing is a really clever computer virus: a little piece of techno-sabotage dreamed up by my competitors. Now, 'fess up, you pixillated refugee from a Disney movie. What is it you want with me, exactly, other than to ruin everything my brother and I have struggled to build here at Databanks and cost thousands of people their jobs?"

"Surely you know that already since you appear to be familiar with the, er, procedure. I believe I must be here simply to, er, ensure that you have—that you appreciate, that is—that you help others to have—a merry Christmas."

"Oh, yeah?"

"I believe so, yes."

"Well, in your own words, then, 'Bah! Humbug!' "

At that point, two separate things happened. One was that red and green lights flashed on and off in front of Scrooge's eyes and when he opened them, he was standing in front of three portals. Two of these were tightly closed with red lights above their thresholds but the third, and nearest, was marked by a button glowing green that bore the legend, Christmas Past.

The second thing that happened, and he only realized this when the lights stopped flashing, was that Monica Banks now stood beside him, her feet lost in mist and her face looking as if, well, as if she'd seen a ghost.

Nine

⌒⌒⌒

Where the door had been there was now a Christmas tree, a large, fresh one, strung with popcorn and cranberries and gilded pinecones.

A man held a little girl up to the top of the tree, where she was placing an angel with a plastic and tinsel halo.

"Angie!" Monica squealed in a voice much younger than her current one. "It's Angie! Our Christmas angel. I used to put her up there every year. Mama and I strung all that popcorn and all those berries and she helped me dip the cones for the tree, too. And Daddy took us over on the ferry boat to the other side of the water and way out into the forest, where a friend of his worked for one of the timber companies so we could cut our tree every year."

Piles and piles of presents sat under the tree, most of them wrapped in paper to please the heart of a child, paper with Santas and elves and snowmen and kittens, paper with reindeer and Christmas trees, little drummer boys and partridges in pear trees, paper with stars and angels and ornaments and candy canes, paper with gingerbread men and bells and holly sprigs and teddy bears. "Can't I open just one now?" the little girl asked.

"You know better than that, princess," her father said. "We have to wait until we get back from Grandma's for the ones under the tree, and then you have to go to sleep so Santa can bring you his gift and fill your stocking."

The father bundled the little girl into her red velvet coat and hat, and after a moment, the mother came from the kitchen bearing a platter large enough to cover her distended belly.

"Come on, hon," the father said.

"I—okay, but let me set this down. I have to make one more trip to the bathroom," she said, and waddled with all speed back into the house before returning to put on her own coat and hat and take up the platter again.

Then they all trundled out into the snow, and the father and daughter hurriedly scooped up big snowballs and threw them at each other, the father laughing delightedly, the daughter shrieking with glee, while the mother, watching each step as best she could, carried the platter to the car. The little girl looked around her neighborhood one last time before getting into the car. The familiar houses had, with the onset of darkness, taken on the aspect of Santa's workshop, each of them strung with bulbs of red, yellow, green, and blue glass shaped like little candle flames. Some houses had Christmas stars on the roof, some had Santas and reindeer teams driving across. Her own yard at least had the snowman she and her daddy had made the day before, though his carrot nose had fallen off.

As the car drove away, Scrooge and Monica watched the snowman wave good-bye to the back of the girl who had created him. The car shushed through snow-muffled streets until Daddy had to stop to put on chains, and after that it clinked and clanked and jingled like sleigh bells.

"I want to see the lights downtown!" the little girl cried, and her parents were only too happy to oblige.

If Scrooge had been awed by the neighborhood light display, the downtown city buildings, comprised of more floors than Scrooge would have thought it possible to pile atop one another, were wonders bedecked with winking glass candles and wrapped like packages. The little girl had to admire the mechanical displays in the store windows—far more elaborate ones than in Scrooge's day—Christmas trains bearing presents in every car and driven by St. Nicholas himself, Christmas parties enacted by windows full of beautifully dressed mannequins, and a completely equipped Santa's toy shop with elves hammering and sawing on wonderful playthings. Christmas music blared out into the streets as if played by invisible orchestras.

Little Monica was most fascinated by the creche in front of a large church whose steeple bore a brightly lit star at its tip. "I hope Santa remembers my Betsey Wetsey," she said to her father in a hushed, excited voice, watching Baby Jesus in Mary's arms as if anxious to see if he dampened his swaddling clothes. "Where will we put the manger when our baby is born?" she asked her parents.

"We won't need a manger," her mother said. "We have your old cradle," and then she gave a little yelp and rubbed her belly. "We'd better get on to Mother's, dear."

"But I was going to use that for Betsey Wetsey," Monica said.

Then, suddenly, the family was on the doorstep of a large house on the outskirts of the city. The door had a big wreath of holly with fat red berries and a fat red bow to match, and when it opened, amazing smells wafted onto the snowy air. Women in silky dresses and frilly aprons bustled around the dining table, filling it with various treats, but Scrooge could only recognize the cranberries, turkey, and dressing.

Much fuss was made over Monica's mother during the meal, and Monica was asked repeatedly by one aunt or uncle or another, "What do you want, Monica, a baby brother or a baby sister?"

She shrugged. "I just want the baby to come out of Momma's tummy so she's not fat anymore and her back doesn't hurt."

Instead of being pleased by her thoughtfulness, her mother blushed. "Monica! That'll be enough of that showing off," she said.

But her daddy ruffled her hair.

Later, everyone sang carols and even later, carol singers came by to sing for them. Monica knew most of the choruses and sang along. They were in the middle of the third chorus of Jingle Bells when Momma suddenly screamed.

"Quick, Tom, get her to the hospital! Her waters just broke!" someone yelled.

Monica's grandmother bustled Monica's mother into the backseat of the car while her father climbed into the driver's seat. Another woman held Monica's shoulders as she watched from the doorway. "Is Momma going to die?" Monica asked, her voice startlingly loud in the snow-muffled air.

"Oh, shut *up!*" her mother screamed. "Drive, Tom."

The little girl in the doorway turned an anxious face to a preoccupied aunt. Later, someone tucked her into bed under a pile of coats.

Scrooge looked at his companion, somewhat at a loss for words, ghostly or otherwise. "Astonishing," he said. "I never married, you know, so I have no idea how such matters are managed. Still, it does seem to me that perhaps the child could have been, you might have been, that is . . ."

"Oh, nowadays they'd probably let me in the delivery room," she said. "But that was back in the fifties. People still thought it was a little tacky for pregnant women to go out in public. Actually, that was something of a false alarm. Mom was in labor over eighteen hours with Doug. I hung out at Grandma's meantime, but Christmas sort of got forgotten because everyone was so worried about Mom and Doug."

"And did you get the doll you wanted?" Scrooge asked.

"I don't remember," Monica said tersely. "Can we go now?"

"Oh, I think there's a bit more to come," Scrooge said.

"It's very clever how you manage this," Monica said a heartbeat later when they stood at yet another door. "I mean, I not only recognize the door to the new house my folks got after Doug was born, I recognize all the little touches that pinpoint things in time."

"Do you?"

"Of course. I knocked that chip in the paint myself when I was ten. And see the wreath? I made that in third grade."

A wreath had indeed appeared since Scrooge and Monica first stood at the door. It was somewhat bedraggled, with the tinsel drooping and the artificial holly lacking leaves in some instances, berries in others, and the bow was much larger on one side than the other and one tail was shorter than the other. For some reason, this made it seem to Scrooge all the more Christmassy.

He opened the door while Monica was still examining the wreath. The rooms inside were quite lavish by the Victorian standards of Scrooge's day. The floor was covered with a tufted carpet, oddly in a single color. Stranger yet was the pink flocked Christmas tree, its star slightly askew at the top, rumpled papers and open boxes beneath it. It stood before a large central window flanked by opulent floral draperies of some material that surely never came from any loom known to Scrooge. Beside this improbable tree was a small box filled with moving pictures similar to those Scrooge had observed in Monica's flat.

Directly in front of this box, Mr. and Mrs. Banks in somewhat slovenly costumes lounged upon a sofa in a pattern that exactly matched the drapes. Before them were arranged legged metal trays, somewhat akin to foreshortened tea carts. Some sort of food sat on sectioned rectangular metal plates upon each tray.

Both people were focused upon the box, which featured a play resembling an extremely sophisticated Punch and Judy show in which a redheaded woman with a loud voice and a Latin-looking man sporting ruffled sleeves were carrying on the traditional Punchian dispute.

In the second room, divided from the first by a shallow archway, at a cherry dining table containing another of the sectioned metal plates, a small boy of perhaps five or six years sat dismembering a doll.

"That was my new Christmas talking doll," Monica told Scrooge with no hint of childlike wistfulness. "I'd forgotten about that. Doug was irritated by the mechanical sound of her voice. He tore her apart, thinking he could improve on it. He did, but he never got the doll back together again. Hardware never was his forte actually, but the voice said, 'Mama' and 'Bye-bye' much more clearly, even though he never got it back in the doll."

"I suppose you were very upset," Scrooge said, desperately trying to think what the first Christmas ghost had said to him.

"No, there I am." She pointed to a corner behind the dining room table where a fat little girl, perhaps twelve years old, with unkempt hair, studied a game board as unblinkingly as a cat at a mouse hole. Scrooge saw something shining on her cheek, but she made not a whimper. "He gave me his Monopoly game. Mom and Dad thought he'd like it because he'd condescended to play it once with a visiting kid. But by that Christmas, he'd already outgrown it. So he got my doll and I got very good at solitary Monopoly."

Mrs. Banks looked fondly back over her shoulder at her son and the doll. "Look at him, Tom," she said to her husband. "Look at how intent he is on fixing that doll. I bet he'll be a great surgeon someday."

"No way," her husband said. "He's hopeless at golf. I took him out with me and all he wanted to do was look into the holes. About lost an eye a couple of times. The boy's dangerous. Whereas Monica's about to *own* the golf course, the way she's going with that game. I think that girl is showing signs of business sense. She asked me to buy a bond for her with the money she got from your folks. I mean to take her to the bank after the holidays and let her do it herself. She's twelve, after all. About time she learned."

"That's all very well, but I worry about her weight. She'll never find a husband as fat as she is. I'm just glad she's learning to type so she'll have something to fall back on."

"The way she's built, she'll always have something to fall back on," the father said with a chuckle at his own joke. "But I wouldn't worry about it. She's still just a kid."

"So it seems you were a person of business even as a young girl," Scrooge said. He could not keep the approval from his voice, for although he had learned that business was not the only thing that was important, he knew that it was nevertheless necessary and practical, if for no other reason than providing one with the means to help the needy.

"Oh, I went through a frivolous period," she said.

And as surely as if they were on a stage, the world around them shifted and they stood in a store full of dresses, along with Mrs. Banks, a bit grayer than she had been in the previous scene, and a Monica who was now a young woman, plump and pretty, flitting from one gossamer gown to the next like a bee from flower to flower.

Scrooge had accepted the changes in their surroundings easily enough so far, but he was beginning to feel a bit miffed, especially when he saw the walls fall away, the curtains become racks of clothing, the carpet change color, the dining table fade and become a sales desk, and most dramatic of all, Mr. Banks and Doug metamorphose into short-skirted, well-coiffed saleswomen.

It seemed to him that it was all very well for such changing about to be magical and mysterious when he was the mortal being led by the ghost; but now that he was the ghost, oughtn't he to be somehow controlling all of this? Then again, how could he, since he had no idea what Monica Banks's previous life had been like?

Monica was somewhat more sanguine about it all. "Nice special effects. I detect Doug's fine hand here."

"Madame, I assure you these are not 'effects' as you call them," Scrooge said sternly, despite his own doubts about their environment. "These are perfectly real supernatural manifestations, as am I."

"Okay, okay, don't get so huffy," she said. "I can't explain how else first Doug and then you could have haunted me or how I came to be here, inside this game of yours, so I have to accept that I am being haunted. But I'll still bet Doug custom-designed this haunting. Who else would make him look so good? He was a *brat* that last Christmas, you know. He screamed and yelled and cried and wouldn't let me play with the doll without saying that he couldn't stand it until Mom made me give it to him just to shut him up. Of course, I was supposed to get it back, but . . . We were supposed to be sharing not trading. I've hated the word *share* ever since then, I think. I never realized that. Hey, maybe you're some kind of therapist-in-costume program Doug made up after all!"

"Madam, I must again remind you that there is no doubt that your brother is dead. This must be distinctly understood, or nothing very wonderful can come of any of this."

"Okay, okay. He's dead. But he was always tricky," she said, looking around the dress shop as if expecting to see her brother hiding under a hem.

"Miss Banks!" Scrooge reprimanded.

"Well, he *was* tricky. I keep expecting him to pop out and say, 'Pay no attention to the man behind the curtain!' "

"Miss Banks, if I may please call your attention to our surroundings," Scrooge said.

The heiress to Databanks appeared somewhat giddy, however, as if she had imbibed too much Christmas punch. "Oh, hey, Ebenezer, I think you can call me Monica now. You seem to be a well-established friend of the family. I mean, you've even met my parents, right?"

"What is this place, Miss—Monica?"

"Nordstrom's, second floor, shoes, lingerie, formal wear. We're in formal wear. That's it. That's the dress I wanted," she said suddenly, pointing to her younger self holding a red, full-skirted frock, much shorter than Scrooge thought seemly, in front of her and admiring her image in the mirror. The gown had a long panel of matching scarlet gauze that draped over the bodice to soften the neckline and made little wings to float behind it. It wasn't the sort of thing a girl would have worn in his day, but Scrooge thought Monica would look quite fetching in it and said so.

"It really was beautiful," she said with a sigh.

At that point an adolescent version of the doll surgeon burst into the store. "Mom, there's the coolest thing at Radio Shack. It's just what I need to get my system going . . ."

"The red dress is too expensive, Monica. How about this lavender strapless? It's more suitable for a girl your age, and it's on sale as well. How much does your equipment cost, Douglas?"

"Oh, never mind!" the teenaged Monica said. "I don't need the dress. I don't have a date, anyway."

"Well, why didn't you say so?" her mother said. "Come on, Douglas. Show me what it is you need."

"He always got everything," Monica Banks told Scrooge angrily. "After he was born, I didn't matter. If he didn't need anything, I could get what I wanted, but he always wanted something to feed his projects. I knew I had to get my own money, so I got jobs after school, and I opened a savings account for college. I kept my job after I graduated high school, and thought if I went to a small, nearby school, I could continue working to buy the extras I might want later."

"Most industrious and highly commendable," Scrooge said.

The store changed. The clothing racks dismantled and sank into the floor in froths of net and silk to reemerge as little white tables surrounded by matching chairs. The sales desk lengthened and acquired a number of spigots and other accoutrements Scooge was less familiar with. Teenaged Monica was behind the counter, her hair pulled back into a high tail, her form clad in a blue dress with a white apron. Two uniformed policemen approached the counter.

"Hi, Jerry, hi, Mike," she greeted them. "Having your usual?"

"Monica, honey, you better come out from behind there and have a seat," the one she'd addressed as Jerry said to her. "We've got some bad news about your parents."

"What?" she asked, fairly vaulting over the counter in her haste to get to the bearers of the news. "What about them?"

The policeman named Mike sat her down. "I'm afraid there was an accident, Monica."

"Accident?"

"A pileup on the highway. The impact must have killed them at once. I'm sure they didn't suffer."

"S-suffer? What about Doug?"

"Your brother was in the backseat, and he was unharmed. He's being taken care of."

"Oh, okay then," she said. "So what can I get you?" and she stood up and started back around the corner again as if they had merely been passing the time of day.

"Monica—"

"Black for you, Jerry, right? And . . ." Then she passed

out right there on top of the Neopolitan ice cream carton, her right hand smashing a stack of sugar cones to the floor as she slipped off the carton and fell the rest of the way, crunching the cones into the linoleum.

"I did not!" Monica said to Scrooge. "I'd never do anything so weak and irresponsible. As I recall it, I worked the rest of my shift and then collected Doug and we made funeral arrangements."

Suddenly, from out of nowhere, an obnoxious buzzer gave a resounding flatulent noise that split the ice cream parlor down the middle. Where the floor had once been, a message that seemed to come from hell now burned in bright red letters: "Incorrect File Name or Pathway: Abort? Retry? Fail?"

"It's Doug!" she said, and yelled to the letters, "Now hear this, brother dear! I remember that day as well as you do. Jerry and Mike came and told me about Mom and Dad and I asked about you and they said you were safe and then I went to get Jerry's coffee and I . . . I . . . I'm pretty sure I finished out the shift. Actually . . ."

The red lights glowed so brightly that Monica and Scrooge were temporarily surrounded by a blaze of red. After a few moments, it twilighted into pink, then golden, and finally, objects and people began to appear within the golden light. Young Monica, still in uniform, sat up on a couch. The policemen and three other women were in the room. Young Doug, now about thirteen, sat dry-eyed under an unlit Christmas tree, playing with a collection of wires and switches, as intent upon them as if he were rebuilding his family.

Wind rattled the windows and stirred the curtains as the girl sat up. "Where am I?" she demanded.

"We're Mr. and Mrs. Christie. Your brother has been staying with us since the—accident, Monica. You're welcome to stay here, too."

"Why should I? We have a home."

"No, we don't," Douglas said. "Mother and Dad rented our house. Nobody's going to rent us a house."

"My word, did you have to go to the workhouse?" Scrooge asked. "Is that how you became as you are?" He would have endorsed such a plan in his earlier days, but since that first haunted Christmas, the very idea filled him with dread.

But the young Monica had turned angrily to her brother.

"Wanna bet?" she said. "I'm nearly twenty. I have a job. I can get another one. I have savings. They'll rent it to us, okay."

"They wouldn't though," Monica told Scrooge. "We had to move into a tiny apartment. Doug was the one who went to college. He got so many scholarships that his education was covered at least. But he was only thirteen and too young to stay on campus, so we lived together in that cramped little place. And you know the hell of it? He didn't even seem to mind.

"In fact, he almost seemed to enjoy himself, even though Mom and Dad were dead and they'd given him everything, *everything*. I realized very fast how much it took to support just the two of us and he never even seemed to care. At least I learned what I needed during that time. Security. Not the kind some boy could offer in a few years. Besides, I didn't know any boys my age, anymore. I knew I needed security right then and I needed to get it by myself so I could count on it. I needed that something to fall back on that Mom was always talking about. Fortunately, I had taken typing and filing in school. So when I saw the ad, I had the skills."

The scene shifted again, this time to an office, much different from Scrooge's old rooms in London. This one was more like the offices he had seen here, but much, much larger. It was so large, and so characterless, so utterly bleak and grim, that it made his old office, with its ledgers and cobwebs and the grate always too cold, seem positively cozy by comparison.

A lone woman, Monica much as she was now but without the gray in her hair, sat at a desk, one hand on a keyboard and the other holding a telephone. "I don't care if it is Christmas, Mrs. Fuentes, you did not pay your taxes this year. It's very unfortunate that your husband ran off with another woman, but the government must be compensated. You have property. Sell that. I can't discuss raising your children with you, Mrs. Fuentes, even if there are eight of them. My business is to see to it that you pay your taxes. Your husband made a great deal of money last year and, filing a joint return, you bear equal responsibility for the tax. No, I'm sorry, but that's the law. Perhaps you should have married someone else."

Scrooge cringed to hear how much this Monica sounded

like himself in the old days. She had said it was Christmas and not a single card, wreath, bit of mistletoe, or greenery brightened that efficient and ruthless place. A stern picture of some American gentleman, no doubt the President, and the flag of the United States on a pole near the entrance were the room's only ornaments.

The calls continued in the same fashion, businesslike, passionless, but stern, very stern. Ah, what the old Scrooge wouldn't have given for a clerk such as Monica Banks!

Finally the lone figure, mouth turned down, curls drooping, shoulders sloping, picked up her bag and descended the steps of the office building to the ground floor, where she waited in the rain at a bus stop.

"I was so tired I forgot the bus wouldn't come on Christmas," she said. "Some holiday. A poor woman works all day long to put food on the table and then has to hike home because the buses use the excuse to let the lazy drivers make everyone walk."

By this time, the younger Monica was indeed walking, block after weary block. She had an umbrella with her, but halfway across the street from the bus stop the wind snapped it inside out and she turned her coat collar up against the weather but walked on, her shoes soaking through and rain streaming down her face. When she arrived at last at her destination, and squooshed in her wet shoes into the lobby of the apartment building, she groaned. There was an "out of order" sign on the lift, which was little more than a floor with an iron fence on three sides and a gate across the front.

From sheer exhaustion, she sat down and cried, her tears almost unnoticable in the general dampness of her person.

Scrooge was about to make some sympathetic remark when the door of one of the first-floor flats opened and a freckle-faced young man, perhaps a year or two older than Doug, stuck his head out. On seeing the wet, weeping Monica, he said, "Ma, one of the neighbors just saw the sign. She looks like she took a bath in her clothes. I think we need some of your special eggnog blend here."

"I don't need *any*thing," Monica said, using her hand to wipe the rain and tears from her face and squishily rising to her feet.

But the young man was as single-minded as she and her brother. "Sure you do, lady. A towel, for one thing." In a moment, a merry-looking woman in a handmade holiday apron thrown hastily over what looked to Scrooge to be some sort of a fuzzy dressing gown handed a cup of the frothy creamy drink to the lad.

"Drink up, lady. It's guaranteed to put roses in your cheeks, Dad always said."

She looked up at him uncertainly, but despite the rain, the walking had been thirsty work and she regarded the beverage with longing.

"It's okay. We're neighbors. I'm Wayne Reilly from 103. That's my mom. What were you doin' out there, anyway? It's raining cats and dogs and besides, everything's closed today."

"Not where I work," she said. "And the buses weren't running, so I had to walk from downtown."

"Tough," he said sympathetically.

But his mother, still standing in the doorway, called, "Don't leave the poor girl sitting in the hallway catching pneumonia while you yammer at her, Wayne," Mrs. Reilly called. "Ask her in. She should dry off and rest before she tackles those steps."

"I have to get home," she said. "I had to leave my little brother alone in the apartment and—"

"And the poor lamb will be lonely for his sister while he's spending Christmas all alone, is it?" Mrs. Reilly asked.

"Well, no, not Doug. I doubt he noticed it was Christmas, except that school's out. Actually, I'm afraid he might have figured out how to recreate the atom bomb and will blow us all up if I don't check up on him pretty soon."

"Not know it's Christmas? What nonsense is that? You have a tree, don't you?"

"Well, no, there wasn't time, and we lost our folks a year ago and when their belongings were sold, I guess the tree sort of went with them."

"Never mind. We have one, and Christmas is more fun with more people. What's your number?"

"Nine-thirteen."

"Wayne, honey, run upstairs and fetch this girl's brother. What's his name? What's your name, for that matter?"

"He's Douglas—Doug, and I'm Monica. Our last name is Banks. But really, Mrs. Reilly, just a quiet—"

"I won't hear of it," she said. "Wayne and I know all about how sad it can be the first Christmas after you're bereaved. We lost my Wilmer five years ago to a heart attack.

Now, Wayne, run along—oh, and ask Monica's brother to bring some dry clothes for her with him, and shoes, too. She can put on something of mine, meantime. Got to get out of those wet things. Now then, Monica, dear, come along and we'll get you dried off and you can rest here on the couch."

The two women disappeared into a room on the side, and when they reappeared a moment later, Monica had a towel wrapped around her wet hair and was wearing over-sized woolly socks and a large Argyle patterned bathrobe in red and black, obviously the property of the late Mr. Reilly. Mrs. Reilly gently forced her to recline on the couch and tucked a hand-crocheted throw over her, then said, "I'll just run and put a few more things in the pot, and we'll have a lovely Christmas dinner together, unless you and your brother had something else planned?"

"No—"

"That settles it then."

Young Monica fell asleep on the couch to the hiss, rattle, and bang of an accordion-shaped object draped with her wet clothing. Scrooge's companion informed him the noisy object was a steam-heating register. Above its clatter was the voice of Mrs. Reilly, singing along with disembodied Christmas carols in the kitchen. The little colored glass candles on the Christmas tree sent soft multihued beams all over the room.

"Who is that singing with Mrs. Reilly?" Scrooge asked, glad for the opportunity to do so, since he had often observed this phenomenon and wondered about it.

Monica gave him a strange look and then said, "Oh,

that's right. You're not supposed to know what a radio is, I guess. It's a device that receives sound waves from a transmitter that carries them from a station. Usually music or news shows but sometimes plays. And of course ads. We never use radio though. Too low tech."

"Low tech?"

"Not technically advanced enough," she said. "I mean, if we can do this," she indicated the scene in which they were standing, "just carrying sound is pretty dull, isn't it?"

"But this isn't a device," Scrooge said. "It's a haunting."

"Yeah, yeah, sure. But there's a device behind this somewhere, let me tell you, and if it's being haunted, it's my dear departed baby brother haunting it. By the way, where is the little dweeb? I don't remember him taking this long."

"You're—um—" Scrooge indicated the sleeping figure on the couch.

"We seem to be seeing a lot of instances where I'm passed out for one reason or the other," Monica complained.

Long minutes continued to tick by on the strange clock with the cat face and the moving tail that the Reillys kept in their living room. Once Mrs. Reilly looked in the living room and started to say, "I wonder where the boys—" and then, seeing Monica asleep, put a finger to her own smiling lips and retreated into the kitchen again.

After a while, the door slammed open and the boys, talking in loud voices about things that made no sense whatsoever to Scrooge, barged into the living room, waking Monica, who sat up rubbing her eyes. "Mom, we're here!"

"As if I couldn't hear you, honey! Hi, Doug, make your-self at home and Merry Christmas."

"Like I was telling you, Wayne," Doug said, "if we adjust this to a lower frequency and—"

"Mom just spoke to you, Doug," Wayne said. "Aren't you going to wish her Merry Christmas back?"

Doug looked as if he'd been jerked awake. "Huh? What? Oh, sure, uh, Merry Christmas—uh—Mom—uh—"

"Reilly," Wayne said.

"Mom Reilly," Doug said, obviously bungling it because he wasn't used to speaking unless it was his own idea.

"He called her *Mom?*" Monica asked Scrooge. "Our mom hadn't been dead but about a year and he was already calling Mrs. Reilly mom."

"She seems a very motherly lady," Scrooge observed.

"Oh, she was, I mean, I guess I could understand it if he called her that *later* because . . . well, later, even I called her Ma Reilly—" Her voice and her indignation died away as Wayne cheerfully tossed some *Popular Mechanics* magazines off a low table in front of the couch and helped his mother set the table with food. A big tureen of savory stew and steaming rolls, plus butter and jam were the Christmas dinner.

"Why, they were too poor for a proper Christmas dinner, too!" Scrooge said.

"Oh, Ma Reilly's stew was better than any old turkey!" Monica said with the first real smile Scrooge had ever seen. "She used plenty of sage and onion and her potatoes were done some special way so even though they were baked in the juices they were still crispy outside, and the carrots! And the celery! I didn't normally like vegetables, but hers were the best. And I have never, in the finest restaurants, tasted bread as creamy and nutty and crusty and delicious as Ma Reilly's. And oh, God, the fudge cake Yule log! Will you look at that thing? It was the most delicious chocolate I've ever had in my life." In the scene before them now, the four people cut into a cylindrical cake topped with sprigs of green and red.

"Well, of course, most women have nothing to do but make a home all day . . ." Scrooge began.

"You're showing your age, old man," Monica said. "Women work all the time now, and even then, a lot of us did. Ma Reilly did. Look at those hands!" Scrooge looked. They were small and had once been shapely but were now rough and red, with big knuckles and nails worn to the quick. "She scrubbed floors and cleaned office buildings to make a living for her and Wayne for years."

"And paid her taxes, I hope," Scrooge said.

Monica, hearing herself mocked, gave him a narrow-eyed frown and turned back to the apartment.

The boys talked nonstop throughout the meal, and young Monica yawned and almost fell asleep in her food. Mrs. Reilly said soothing things to her and when the dinner was over, Wayne helped her clear the table. Monica looked surprised when the Reillys dragged Doug with them to the kitchen, insisting that he help and let his sister rest. Young Monica smiled gratefully.

"I'd forgotten about that, but you know, I think that was

the first time anyone ever insisted Doug do anything for my sake," she said.

While the girl napped, the dishes were done. Once, Mrs. Reilly slipped back into her bedroom and there were rustlings and a satisfied humming of "We Three Kings" while in the kitchen the boys sang, "We Three Kings of Orientar/ Tried to smoke a rubber cigar./It exploded, it went *bang!*/ We two kings of Orientar . . ." Then Mrs. Reilly bustled back across the living room, with a surreptitious glance at Monica, and with a backhanded toss, deposited a present beneath the branches of the Christmas tree.

She had only been back a moment when Wayne excused himself to use the rest room, and his mother asked Doug if he would use his long arms to put away the mixing bowls that went on the top shelf.

Wayne made a great show of going into the bathroom and turning on the water; then, with the posture of a soldier fleeing the enemy, with many commando-like glances over his shoulders, dived into the corner of the room he shared with his mother where he kept his special cache of equipment and projects. His mother asked many questions of Doug in the kitchen while Wayne made his selection and wrapped it in a bit of used paper and ribbon from that his mother had carefully saved from the wastepaper baskets of her employers, Scrooge guessed, by the way the creases were smoothed. Then, with more duckings and evasions of imaginary enemies, he concealed his secret dispatch from the enemy in the forest that happily was planted there in his living room. Then, whistling the Three Kings carol, he rejoined his mother and Doug in the kitchen with every appearance of wide-eyed innocence.

"Time for presents now, Ma!" he said.

Monica roused herself. "We should be going. I have to go to work again tomorrow."

"Nonsense, dear. Do stay while we open gifts. Wayne, you be Santa."

Wayne delivered Mrs. Reilly's gift first. It was a bracelet woven from brightly colored electrical wires. Mrs. Reilly reacted as if the red wires were strings of rubies, the blue were sapphires, and the yellow were rare canary diamonds. Wayne got handmade mittens and a scarf that was made out of many colors and stretched a full three yards long. He wound it around his neck so many times his head disappeared, then tried to tie Monica and Doug together in it, until his mother told him to get the other gifts.

He shoved a package at Doug. "Here. I thought this would go with, you know, what we were talking about."

Doug unwrapped it. "What is it?" Scrooge asked.

"I don't know." Monica answered. "Never did. Doug liked it, though." He was describing in great technical length to Wayne how it could be used when Wayne handed a package to the young Monica.

This was wrapped in the best of the creased paper, with poinsettias, and had tissue inside. The girl lifted from it a collar made of lace.

"I know the girls don't wear those much these days, but you have such a lovely, slender neck—like I used to. I thought it would suit you," Mrs. Reilly said.

Young Monica put it on over the argyle bathrobe and stroked it flat. "It's beautiful."

"It's from Ireland. My mother-in-law gave it to me when Reilly and I first started going together. Her mother made it."

Young Monica smiled rather shyly before she stiffened her shoulders and said, "I think my clothes will be dry now, and I need to get to bed so I'll be ready for work in the morning. Thank you for a lovely evening. Come along, Doug."

"Later, Sis. I wanna talk some more with Wayne."

"You can do that tomorrow, Douglas," Mrs. Reilly said. "I have to go to work tomorrow, too, you know. Every day can't be like Christmas, I'm afraid. But you must come back whenever you wish."

They saw another Christmas in that same apartment, and now it had a television Wayne had earned at his job in an appliance store. He and Doug were still as talkative as ever, but Mrs. Reilly looked a bit older and Monica left sooner.

Throughout the building, rock and roll music blared from Christmas parties elsewhere and on the television screens, with the sound off, scenes of war were interspersed with those of entertainers singing carols.

"It seems a strange thing to watch a war, however far-away, at Christmas," Scrooge said.

"Mrs. Reilly was a little peculiar," Monica said. "She said that she sort of felt that, by keeping the set on and remembering the boys, they'd be sharing our Christmas in some way. She got stranger as she got older. Once Wayne and

Doug got the company running, Wayne sent her to some fancy home in Florida, I think."

"You look as if you're about to cry," Scrooge suggested wistfully. He had seen very little emotion from her, if truth be told, and by this stage in his own haunting, he was already in tears.

"No way," she said, blowing her nose hard and turning away from the image of Mrs. Reilly beaming over the fudge cake log. "It was just so silly, her giving me that lace collar like that. I never wore the thing, of course. Anyone could tell you I'm not the lacy type"

"Of course not," Scrooge said hastily.

"It just seems a waste, is all."

"You could give it to charity, I suppose," Scrooge said. "If you didn't think that was too much, along with the fruit-cake."

"Some people *like* fruitcake," she said. "I just don't happen to be one of them."

The apartment building was fading back into the tax office again, and Christmas after Christmas rushed past, always with Monica on the telephone, making threats, ruining people's holidays. Waiting for her at home were Doug and, usually, Wayne, who sometimes brought a special treat his mother had made. The boys were always working on a project.

"This is getting monotonous, young lady," Scrooge said. "Had you no private life?"

"Boyfriends, you mean?"

"Suitors, certainly."

"You'd be surprised how quickly guys lose interest when they find out you work for the IRS, and personnel aren't allowed to date within the department." She shrugged. "It's different now, but I'm not exactly jailbait anymore. Once Doug got a bit older, I stopped coming home for Christmas altogether and just stayed at the office and collected my double time. He and Wayne were usually too engrossed in their technical stuff to pay me any mind."

But once more they were standing in the cramped apartment and Monica came up the stairs, opened the door, threw down her purse, and sprawled in the broken-springed easy chair sitting near the door. Her eyes closed wearily and didn't see that now the two young men were indeed paying rapt attention to her.

Wayne nudged Doug. "Go on. You tell her. She's your sister."

Doug raised his eyebrow and shook his head. He was trying for a disdainful look, but to Scrooge, he looked uncustomarily daunted.

He cleared his throat, and his Adam's apple bounced up and down. He turned away.

"Go *on*," Wayne urged.

Doug shook his head. "You."

Wayne sighed. "Monica, Doug and I have something to tell you."

The woman in the chair half opened one eye. "What?" she asked, as if expecting the answer to be that they'd broken or ruined something costly and irreplacable.

"We're going into business together. We have a great idea, and it'll make us bigger than IBM, and—"

"And what about school?"

"We didn't either of us go back for spring semester. Our math prof is supplying some of the capital we need, but we plan to buy him out when we start showing a profit."

"What does your mother say to this?"

Wayne developed a fascination with the laces of his shoes. "It's partly for her sake I want to move out and get this going. She can't go on working much longer, Moni. Her arthritis has really been bothering her this winter, and she's too tired to do anything after work anymore. If we're all together, and she's where Doug and I are working all day, I can look after her better."

"Oh, sure. Like you and Doug ever notice anything that's going on around you while you're working. What's wrong with you working in your apartment? I suppose you like the Cheetos better up here?"

"It's inadequate, Monica," Doug put in abruptly. "Surely you can see that. Wayne is oversimplifying a bit. We're going to need staff—a manufacturing facility, as well as idea people and work space, in addition to living quarters. We've actually pretty much moved in there now, but we didn't want to say anything to you about it until we had our feet on the ground."

"Doug didn't want you to worry," Wayne said.

"Doug didn't want to have to listen to my reasons why it's a silly idea and I think he's suddenly got delusions of grandeur. What do you boys know about running a business?

Do you know how many great ideas are sold for nothing to someone with the capital to realize them? Do you know how many businesses go under in the first year? How many expand too rapidly and overextend themselves? Do you even know the sort of tax liability you'll be looking at with these people you're speaking of hiring—social security, health benefits, unemployment . . ."

"We thought we'd hire people on contract and make up to them in stock options what the job lacks in benefits," Doug said as if he was talking about the merits of different television channels.

"We also thought maybe you'd like to come in with us and help us manage the business," Wayne said.

"That would be a conflict of interests," she told them. "And besides, if I did that, and gave up my job, who would you turn to when you fail?"

"Thanks, Sis," Doug said. He surprised her by giving her a kiss on the cheek as the two of them left.

"Apparently they only stayed around long enough to ask me," Monica Banks, now CEO of the company she'd predicted would fail, told Scrooge. "I never actually noticed that before."

"You apparently failed to notice a great many things," he said.

At their feet, more letters lit up. The heading was "Program Manager" and the box checked said "Review."

Whether or not it did Monica any good, Scrooge could not have said, but it was a revelation to him.

The sixties, with loud music and strangely costumed people called hippies campaigning for everything from the rights of the descendants of the former African slaves to free love, which Scrooge supposed had something to do with being opposed to streetwalkers. Monica's comments were terse. "They pretended to be poor to avoid paying taxes because they didn't approve of one thing or another. As if the government could consult every citizen on every decision before taxing them for it!"

"What a sensible attitude, my dear. I take it you disagree strongly with those early colonials who dumped valuable tea in one of your eastern harbors then?"

There was more about the war they had seen briefly on television. "A very costly mistake," she said, and Scrooge, seeing the corpses of young men being zipped into body bags, once more regretted a remark he had made in the old days about diminishing the excess population. "But it is over with," Monica continued, "a good twenty years ago now, and I don't know why people don't just get over it and get on with life."

Scrooge was still looking at the body bags.

There was also something called the sexual revolution, which Scrooge found rather shocking. Monica was a bit wistful over that one. "One reason you never saw me with a boyfriend is that they never lasted till Christmas. Either I broke up with him because I didn't think he was worth buying a gift for, or he broke up with me to avoid buying a gift. I don't want you to think I never . . ."

"My dear, that is your own affair—sorry, bad choice of words—your own private matter entirely," Scrooge hastily assured her. "My own ghosts and I went into courtship with one significant young lady, but it never strayed beyond the bounds of decorum."

The bluestockings had apparently been successful with putting forward their agenda in this time also, and something called women's liberation had taken hold. Monica was skeptical of that. "There's still a glass ceiling, you know," she said with a sniff. "The only good thing about it is that it came along in time for the current economy, where it takes both members of a marriage working to support themselves. And some women have used it for every sort of crybabyishness. Demanding maternity leaves and paid child care, for instance, and those silly girls who get themselves knocked up and then want the government to pay for it."

"Are there no workhouses? Are there no jails?" Scrooge asked with a ruefulness lost on her.

And then, suddenly, there was a grave and afterward, in a tastefully appointed room, a young woman with a sonorous voice began reading a will, " 'I, Douglas Banks, being of sound mind and body . . .' "

"Get me out of here, Scrooge. I don't want to go through this again," Monica said, and then she was gone. Through the frame that customarily separated his rather peculiar spirit world from Monica's corporeal one, Scrooge could see her once more curled up on her couch, the pillow held before her protectively.

Ten

⟨∞⟩

Scrooge was wondering what to do next when the frame was suddenly filled with a collection of faces.

"Do me next," Curtis said.

"Me, too," Melody added. "I've always wanted to do that."

"How do we get in?"

"I'm sure I don't know," Scrooge said, looking from one face to the other.

He felt a warm glow on his face and shoulders and looked up to see a golden light that read "Program Manager" lit over his head, with choices reading "Escape," "Help," and "Enter" shining with a ruby glow.

"Geronimo," John said, and twiddled something that clicked. The "Enter" button above Scrooge blinked from ruby to gold and a moment later John was standing inside the frame, beside Scrooge. Very quickly he was joined by the others.

"We saw all about Money Banks and her unhappy past,"

Harald said. "Now do us. We want to see each others' Christmases past."

"Do you just do Christmas, or will you do Hannukah and Kwanzaa and Yule and Saternalia as well?" Miriam asked.

Scrooge was embarrassed. "I beg your pardon, madam, but I'm afraid I don't know what those are. I only know Christmas, and frankly, I learned about it rather late in life."

"Hmmph, doesn't show much cultural diversity," Sheryl said.

"He's a Victorian Englishman, for heaven's sake, Sheryl, whaddaya want from him?" Phillip said.

"This is a very Eurocentric program or virus or whatever it is, is all I'm saying," Sheryl said.

"Haunting, miss," Scrooge said, a little wearily now.

"Ex*cuse* me?"

"It's a haunting, miss."

"Then why does it have a program manager and a lotta choices up over our heads?" she demanded.

"On the other hand," Harald said, "if it's a standard program or virus, why does it have us standing around inside of it instead of directing it from our seats. I don't recall putting on any special VR equipment, do any of you?"

"Good point," said John, Curtis, Phillip, and David simultaneously as they nodded and looked around them.

"I just think something supernatural wouldn't smack so much of the dominant culture," Sheryl insisted.

"That being in this case, the dead? Christmases past?" Harald said. "Hmmm . . ."

"Look, Mr. Scrooge here is a literary device—" Miriam began.

"I beg your pardon, young lady!" Scrooge said indignantly.

"Well, possibly based on real life, but based on it by Mr. Dickens, who may have been dominant culture but was one of the big social consciences of his time."

"So?"

"So, Mr. Scrooge is definitely on board to teach Monica something, and apparently, us, too, just like in the book."

"Yeah," Melody said, looking around. "Yeah, and it's really cool and everything, except why do I share Monica's feeling that this whole milieu has been designed by Doug? You sure Doug Banks didn't put you up to this, Eb, honey? I mean, Monica did say she'd seen him, and he'd mentioned you were coming, right?"

"Presumption on his part," Scrooge said. "I was never asked. Naturally, I would have been happy to accede to any reasonable request, although being dead was something of an obstacle to receiving or executing—excuse the terminology please—such a request."

"And only one way you got here after being dead and everything, into this particular place, no matter who designed the environment," Curtis said slowly. "Ladies and gentlemen, we all know Doug Banks at least by reputation and while we had to *think* he was God while he was boss, actually, he was just a very hot tekkie millionaire. He couldn't have brought Ebenezer Scrooge back from the dead."

"Maybe he didn't. I'm not convinced this thing is real," Sheryl said. "Come on, Scrooge, I want to see my past. I was real misunderstood. My therapist can tell you all about it. My mama had three husbands and my daddy had four wives and I have sisters and brothers I have never even met. Our family Christmases were a nightmare. I got to where I talked to my 'puter 'cause it was the only one I could count on not getting divorced and moving out on me."

"That's touching," Curtis said, nodding. "That's very touching. I grew up in the International District and my father really wanted me to go into importing."

"That's your tragic story?"

"That's it. Except, when I was a kid, we never got into Christmas as much as I always wanted to, because we were Buddhist. I really think the old man was just too cheap."

"My mom left us and my dad drank," John said.

"I kept wishing my mother *would* leave us," Harald sighed, "but she never did, so *I* have to drink."

"Hey, we're talking serious childhood traumas here," David said. "Speaking for myself, I was just so damn brilliant, nobody in my family ever—sobs here, deep sobs—understood me."

"Sorry," Harald replied. "I'm an insensitive brute. I know that. It's spoiled *all* my Christmases."

"Ahem," Scrooge said. "There is, as you see, only one door," he pointed to the portal that had opened up under a sign that now said, "Christmas past, continued." "Shall we?"

They did and were whisked immediately into a maelstrom of activity. People in the briefest possible costumes scurried to and fro bearing sacks and gift-wrapped packages while the sun beat down mercilessly upon their heads.

"I don't understand," Scrooge said. "Where are we?"

Miriam had paused at a machine that dispensed newspapers. "We're in Seattle, that's perfectly obvious, in the middle of Westlake Plaza between Nordstrom's, the Bon, and the Westlake Mall. You can tell by the fancy brickwork here, see, Scrooge. They don't let cars drive here."

Scrooge had by now taken in the cars rushing along the nearby streets and found them a bit unnerving. "What if one of them—ahem—should disobey? Would we all be killed instantly?"

Miriam shrugged. "Nope, but he'd get a hell of a ticket. Look here, guys, this is so bogus. We're not in any Christmas past at all. This is last July."

Melody shrieked, "Eek! I knew it!" Everyone looked where she was now pointing, much, Scrooge remembered, as the bony hand of the Ghost of Christmas Yet to Come had pointed at his own gravestone. There, in front of the plaza, was another Melody, this one clad in a red velvet costume of the utmost brevity, paradoxically trimmed with fur, long, green-banded stockings that stopped about a foot short of the hem of her garment, and curly-toed slippers.

"Oh, is *that* the elf gig you were telling me about?" Sheryl asked her with a giggle. "You're right. Gruesome in the extreme."

"I don't understand at all," Scrooge said. He was not

happy about this. He was almost certain neither Marley nor any of the dignified ghosts that had attended him had been subjected to large groups of people who spoke their own language—rather like being a tour guide in a country stranger to you than to those you were guiding, it seemed to him. Not entirely cricket, that.

"It's Christmas in July, old man," Harald said, attempting to clap him on the ghostly shoulder. Didn't work.

"I distinctly remember that Christmas arrives in December, on the twenty-fifth to be precise," Scrooge said.

"Ah, maybe in London, old bean, and maybe in the long ago, but in America, we have better merchandising schemes than that. Christmas in July is a fine old retail custom that capitalizes on the prime emotion Christmas awakens in many middle-class working Americans."

"Joy?" Somehow, Scrooge knew that wasn't the right answer.

"Terror," Harald said. "Terror of being so stressed-out you won't do anything right; terror of not meeting all your obligations; terror of not providing the best Christmas pageant ever; terror of—heaven forbid!—not having your heart warmed in some way or significantly warming the hearts of your family with a monumental pile of gifts under a tree worthy of Martha Stewart."

"And don't forget, Harald, be fair," Melody put in, "the retailers are terrified, too. In small, touristy towns throughout the land, they quake between tourist season and Christmas for fear the sales figures won't be up during the holiday season and their businesses will, like, croak. Sometimes even the major stores overstock during the summer when locals avoid large population centers because they're so full of tourists. So businesses entice customers downtown by appealing to the virtue of the customer who wants to shop early and avoid the Christmas rush by participating in the Christmas in July rush."

"Fine institution," Phillip said ruefully, going into the mall where little trays and tables of things were set out in front of stores. "Another good excuse to get rid of old merchandise during a sale and make way for the good stuff they get for the real Christmas. Also a way to get rid of old ornaments and seasonal items that didn't sell last year."

Scrooge looked at the many beautiful beaded and sequined, quilted, and tufted ornaments, not to mention the handblown glass ones. They were lovely in design but rather poorly made. Each of them said "China" on a small white tag someplace on its surface. "I had no idea China was such a Christmassy place," he confessed. "I thought it was wholly comprised of opium dens and sinister men with long mustaches and ladies with tiny, bound feet. And—er—dragons; that sort of thing."

Curtis rolled his eyes, but Miriam said soothingly, "Remember, he's a Victorian Englishman, Curtis, and consider the source. The literature of the day was full of that stereotype, and I'll bet Mr. Scrooge wasn't exactly widely traveled." She cocked an eyebrow at him.

"I took the train to Manchester once," he declared stoutly.

"See what I mean?" she told Curtis.

"I'm not a complete dweeb, Miriam, I know that," Curtis said. "It's just that this kind of trash really annoys me, Scrooge." He wasn't talking about Scrooge's words, he was holding up a Christmas ornament. "Do you know that a lot of this stuff for the holiday of joy and family and giving and warmth and all like that is made by slave labor? I had a cousin at Tianamen Square . . ."

Scrooge tried to look politely inquiring, and Melody leaned over and whispered in his ear, "There was a terrible massacre there where the students were protesting for democracy and the government troops shot them and ran over them with tanks."

"Good heavens," Scrooge said, and was ashamed for having felt for so long that China, at least, was one place on earth where one did need to decrease the excess population. Apparently all he had heard about how little Chinamen valued life was untrue, for Curtis seemed most genuinely upset.

"Some of those students have never come out of prison," Curtis told him. "And they, along with other people in disfavor with the government for one reason or the other, are locked up in factories no better than those of your own day and tortured and humiliated into mass-producing this sort of trinket." He tossed the ball back into its basket. "I find it hard to believe anyone can get into such an altruistic mood as people are supposed to at Christmas when surrounded by junk made by slave labor."

"I do see your point, dear boy," Scrooge said.

"Oh, hey, Curtis, all that altruism and joy is exaggerated,

anyway. We all know that the suicide rate is higher at Christmas than other times." This was from Melody. "Family deaths, too. Since my Grandma died at Christmas five years ago, I keep noticing how many people get divorced or lose a mom or dad or a kid at Christmas. And it seems like there's always some big disaster like a flood or an earthquake or a fire that wipes out a bunch of people every year."

"Crime's worse, too. In fact, I think we can agree we'd all be better off without it," David growled. "So let's get out of here. I wore my HO-cubed sweatshirt tonight and I'm sweltering."

"You can't be sweltering," Sheryl told him sternly. "Here we're as much ghosts as Mr. Scrooge. Right?"

"He's real suggestible, Sheryl, you know that," Melody said with a kindly look at the marketing manager.

Scrooge had wandered away from them and was listening to more disembodied Christmas music coming from a variety of cards, bell ornaments, and lights. None of it had a very good tone, but he thought it was a lovely idea. Perhaps Doug Banks could have made it sound more like music if he had lived long enough, in the same way he had improved the voice on his sister's doll.

"Well, I for one am disappointed," Sheryl said. "I thought we were going to have profound revelations here and all we did was come back to the sale I avoided the first time."

"I wish I had," Melody said. "If I hadn't needed the money so bad, I'd never have taken the job. All those guys who thought they were being cute trying to get me to sit on *their* laps while they told me what they wanted for Christmas. *Gruesome.*"

Scrooge suspected from the expressions on the faces of many of the other people in elf costumes that Melody's feelings were shared by her coworkers. Besides, unfamiliar as he was with how this city customarily celebrated Christmas (except for the glimpses he'd had into Monica Banks's past), this setting lacked the proper feeling entirely. There were no street decorations, no wreaths on doors, no Christmassy feel at all to the sale.

All he saw around him were tawdry trinkets made, according to these people, possibly by slave labor. Baskets full of shopworn merchandise. Lights that blinked furiously enough to give anyone a headache, if the tinny carols that came from no musical instrument ever invented by God or man had not already done so. Unseasonable weather and harried people. He and Christmas both were completely out of place on this hot summer day in this hot little indoor village within a city. The air was not as sooty or foggy as his London, but it was somehow less wholesome for being confined.

Harald and Miriam caught his eye and drew the attention of the others to him. "Hey, you guys, I think Mr. Scrooge is about ready to say The Line."

"I beg your pardon?" Scrooge said.

"You know," Miriam prompted, "*the* line, your famous one—first word, sounds like a lamb?"

"Bah!" said Scrooge, who'd absolutely adored guessing games since that first Christmas, when, while being haunted into attending his nephew's party, he'd started playing Scattergories.

Miriam and the others were making encouraging motions with their hands, "That's it. 'Bah!' and . . . help him out, gang. I think he agrees with us about Christmas in July. Christmas in July, Mr. Scrooge. Whaddaya think?"

"I think that while the spirit of Christmas should be in one's heart all year long, the celebration of Christmas proper should bloody well stay in December, where it belongs, and Christmas in July is nothing but—"

And one and all chorused together, "Humbug!"

After that, they had a much merrier time. They were laughing at everything, laughing so much they would, had anyone else been able to hear or see them, have been thrown out by one of the uniformed guards.

Sheryl brought them all back to reality. "We got work to do, and we'd best get back to it. How do you suppose we get out of this thing?"

By now they were at an escalator. Above it was a sign with a panel of buttons.

"Hit 'Escape'?" Melody suggested.

"Right," Phillip said and jumped straight up, yelled, "Slam dunk," and hit the sign.

Instantly they were back in their offices, though Scrooge still regarded them from the inside of the computer. "Excuse me," he said. "There's a small problem."

"I'll say," Sheryl said. "Would you mind getting out of the way, old buddy? I gotta kick some butt here, and I can't do it with you hogging, or is that haunting, the pathways."

"I'd be happy to oblige," Scrooge said. "But I have a feeling we are all bound together in this adventure until the end."

Sheryl tapped impatiently at her keyboard. Curtis was pulling wires and plugs, to no avail.

"I have a feeling you're right," Melody said. "I guess since you just did Christmas Past you must be ready for Christmas Present, huh?"

"Yes, thanks to you, I have in some measure been enlightened as to the nature of my haunting, but I still have one or two concerns."

"Which are?"

"Miss Banks is no longer awed by me, you see. She's grown quite used to the idea that I am Ebenezer Scrooge of another century and that her brother is somehow behind my manifestation. I fear that I will not be able to make her respect my message. I do not wish to storm about and make demands. That's not in the least Christmassy. I wish to inspire her to open her heart."

"Her alleged heart," Phillip said.

"No problemo, baby," John said. "All you gotta do is morph."

"I beg your pardon?"

"Metamorphose into another shape," Melody explained. "It's easy."

"It is?"

"Just try. Pick an image, and change yourself into it."

Scrooge studied on the problem and as he did so, his hair bundled itself into a braided bun, and a little cap appeared upon it, he grew an ample bosom and a lap and found to his alarm he was wearing a queenly gown.

"You never know who's going to turn out to be a cross-dresser do you?" Harald observed to no one in particular.

"That was very good, Scroogie," Melody said. "Queen Victoria ought to impress the stuffing out of Money Banks."

"If I may just say something," Dave from marketing said, clearing his throat. "Image is my business, and I somehow don't think Her Maj is really, you know, quite the look you're shooting for."

Scrooge focused gratefully on the young man. "How astute of you, my dear boy. If you could just tell me what look I am shooting for, I'd be ever so pleased."

"Well, in the book and most of the plays and even the takeoffs, Christmas present is this big, abundant looking guy, kind of like a cross between Dionysus—"

"That's the pagan god of wine and merriment," Miriam put in.

"—and a Victorian Santa. You want big, larger-than-life, merry, jolly, red-cheeked, red-haired if you can manage it, and—er—flowing robes, some snappy holly trim, maybe a garland for your head—or do you guys think that's a little too much?"

"No, that's *perfect*, Dave," Melody said, clapping her hands as Scrooge turned slowly to show her his new regalia. He even felt different. He was naturally inclined to kindliness and jollity since the Christmas of his own metamorphosing, but now he felt expansive, grand, truly merry, as if there was nothing in the whole world that time and love and the magic of Christmas could not change. Even though he knew, in his heart of hearts, that this was utter claptrap, poppycock, and humbug.

Of course, changing the world took not only those qualities but much hard work, dedication, energy, time, and money from every soul who would seek to make a real improvement. In this guise he did not care. And the task did not seem so onerous. He could light not only one candle in the darkness, he could light hundreds.

"Sic 'er, Eb, I mean, Ghost of Christmas Present," Harald said.

"Yeah, break a leg," Melody said.

"Save me a turkey leg if you go to any really good feasts, will you?" Dave asked.

"And eggnog. I love eggnog," Phillip added.

But Scrooge had turned to focus on the room where Monica Banks once more lay rolled up like a wreath on her sofa.

He had an idea then. He didn't bring her inside the computer. Such was his grandness in this guise that he was able to enlarge his surroundings to encompass the whole room, the whole city, the whole building, and the whole world.

Eleven

GILLS

Monica smelled gingerbread, mincemeat, pine needles, and cedar logs burning in the fireplace. She sat up, rubbed her aching back, and looked around her suspiciously. The apartment looked normal enough, but from beneath her office door, lights twinkled red, green, gold, and blue. "Oh, no," she groaned. "Showtime." She remembered this part in the story. This was where Christmas Present was hiding in another room, waiting to lower the boom on—Scrooge. But Scrooge was who would be waiting. And he knew she knew. So that was all right. It was a waste of time, of course, but she felt a little more in control. It was like that guided dreaming stuff someone had mentioned at one of her product launch parties.

She had obviously guided Scrooge through her early life, wanting him to understand the choices she'd made and that she wasn't really such a bad person, after all. And now—and now, well, she wished they could just skip the whole thing. Just at this moment, her life was a bit of a nonevent, personally speaking, which was the only criteria Scrooge seemed willing to accept.

But she was finally in control. No more calling people up dunning them on Christmas, hearing them whining, making excuses, or more rarely, cussing her out. She was wealthy, she had a friend in the government, a new project that was going to revolutionize computerized communications, and a staff that was, if not loyal, at least bound to her by ironclad contracts. Finally, she was in the driver's seat. It was her office. She could go right back to sleep if she wanted to.

Then it started. Somehow, something had gotten into the loud speakers in her room and over and over the tape played computer-generated cat meows singing, "We Wish You a Merry Christmas."

It was more than she could bear.

She jumped up from the couch, threw the pillow aside, stormed to the office door, and threw it open. Some big fat guy in a bathrobe was sitting at her computer. He looked stoned. "Who are you?" she demanded.

"I am the Ghost of Christmas Present," he said, in a booming but strangely familiar voice. "Come in and know me better," he said.

"Just what do you think you're doing at my terminal?" she demanded.

"Why, I'm not doing anything. You and your company, however, are sending a universal message of best wishes for Christmas and all holidays the people of the world hold in their hearts, with peace on earth, good will to men—"

"How about women?"

"Everybody," the fat guy said with a maniacal Santa Claus laugh as he stood and threw his arms open. "Everybody." This wasn't Scrooge. This guy was about seven feet tall.

"Look," she said, "I'm just not in the mood for Christmas this year, okay? I have a lot on my mind. Tell Doug I really appreciate the trouble he took to come and haunt me but—"

"Hurry," he said, opening the office door so that an icy blast laden with snow swept in, which was impossible because there was a great deal more building between her and the outdoors. "Our sleigh is waiting."

"Sleigh? What sleigh?"

But sure enough, sleigh bells jingled. She turned to look back at her television set, but all she saw was the reflection of her own back.

She walked over to the door. "I am in charge," she said to herself. "I am in control, and I can do what I want. I am the boss."

The wind snatched the door handle from her fingers and pushed her out the door, slamming it behind her and leaving her outdoors. The hall no longer existed. She was out on the grounds, in the drive in front of her building where the wind swirled the snow so fast she could scarcely see. A great red velvet cape fell across her shoulders, enveloping her. In front of her was an old-fashioned sleigh, red with gilt trim and two handsome dapple-gray Percherons ready to pull at the command of the fat guy, who was in the driver's seat.

"Get in and know me better, child," the fat guy said. She

knew without trying it that the building was locked behind her, and she was fairly certain no one would answer the buzzer. She did not have her key with her, of course. And she had kicked off her shoes when she lay down on the couch. Getting frostbite was no way to start a new year.

"Okay," she said, "but you bring me back when I say so, understand? Kidnapping is a federal offense."

The big, fat guy laughed as if she'd been particularly witty and clucked to the horses. They trotted forward, their feathered feet plopping in the snow and their bells jingling.

"So where are we going?" she asked finally. "To some darkened theater where you force me to watch *It's a Wonderful Life* over and over again?"

"If you didn't have to work, where would you have wanted to go?" the driver asked her. Now that she was closer to him, she thought there was something Scroogish about him after all, in spite of the fact that he was massive and fleshy instead of stringy and spare.

Okay, she'd play his silly game. The point in the story was that Scrooge didn't have any friends, wasn't it? Well, she had plenty of friends. Important friends. "Senator Johansen's house, please."

The driver just nodded and took a shortcut through the woods on her grounds. Although it was still nighttime, the sky was ivory with snow and alive with creatures startled awake by the storm. A family of deer stopped nuzzling aside drifts to find grass and watched as the sleigh drove past, and squirrels chattered in the trees while whole flocks of birds swept like curtains from air to ground and ground to air again, their wings black amid the twisting snow.

He showed her tracks of animals she didn't know could be found in the city: foxes, beavers, coyotes, and even the paw prints of a passing mountain lion. Twin points of illumination beamed through the trees and, as the sleigh approached, became miner's lights strapped over the stocking caps of a pair of laughing people on cross-country skis. Obviously besotted with each other, the pair skated past the sleigh near enough to touch it. Their socks and sweaters were patterned with reindeer, their foreheads beaded with sweat, and their conversation about mulled cider and turkey sandwiches when they returned home.

"They're trespassing," she said, looking after them as long as she could, fascinated by the fluid movement of their skis. "Next thing you know it'll be snow machines."

"Next thing you know this will all be gone," the spirit beside her said.

"The snow?"

"I was referring to the trees and the animals but the snow as well. Enjoy it before it turns to slush."

She knew this was sound advice, so she faced forward again. He was intent on his driving and wouldn't see. She stuck her tongue out to catch a flake.

The trees rose high above them, alive in the ivory night with shadow and flicker, bright eyes, the twitch of a tail, the flirt of a wing. She hadn't a clue where they were. She had no idea this road ran back here. She realized on paper that she owned this entire woods and she saw it every day from the parking lot when she approached the building, but until now she had never spent any time in it. "It's really beautiful here, isn't it?" she said to the ghost.

"Useless though," he said. "A lot of old dead trees when it could be expensive high-rise multiunit housing."

Before she could respond to that, they pulled out of the wild section of the woods and emerged onto a wide, tree-lined street full of large, stately homes. At the opposite end from where they were was a little sentry station where an armed guard protected the privacy of the residents, and grids with sharp spikes shredded the tires of unwanted interlopers.

The senator's home, Monica knew, was set far back from the road with a grassy park of a lawn in front of it. Tonight she didn't recognize it. Soaring trees, larger than those she and the spirit had just driven through in her forest, stood thickly beyond the gate, every one of them twinkling with lights. As the sleigh drove down the broad avenue between the towering trees, Monica saw that they weren't growing out of the ground but that each was supported by an ingenious scaffolding also decorated with lights. It was extremely beautiful, but the birdless, squirrelless dead branches lit with electric bulbs made her feel a little sad for no reason she could think of.

She was disappointed the valets who were parking the cars couldn't see what she arrived in. She thought she'd like to remember this sleigh business as a great way to make an entrance at another party—one where she was visible.

This must be Christmas night, she thought, because the

ghost or ghosts was/were supposed to come on three con-
secutive nights. And of course, Bob had asked her to dinner
last night, so it wouldn't have been when he'd already
planned a large celebration at his own home.

"I knew that the senator lived here," she said to the
Ghost of Christmas Present, "but I had no idea his place
was so close to Databanks."

"It isn't," the ghost said. "This is a magic sleigh, of course,
borrowed particularly for the occasion. So we used a little
sleight of hand, you might say."

"I would have preferred that you hadn't," she said, rolling
her eyes, and she climbed down, clutching the warm red
velvet cloak around her as they entered the house. She
stroked the velvet and wondered why she had never bought
one for herself. It had a wonderful feel and you didn't need
to worry about being well-dressed. She felt like some kind
of a Christmas spy there in her gray workout togs with the
cloak's soft folds brushing her like some large, affectionate
cat.

A Christmas tree decked in gold and white stood sentinel
in the front hallway, but the butler did not offer to take the
cloak, nor to relieve the Ghost of Christmas Present of the
wreath he wore like a hat. The two of them swept into the
dining room, its arched doorway flanked by more Christmas
trees, these in pink and silver, to see the heavily laden table
and the right-wing government leaders from western Washington, as well as the conservative Christian leaders, plus
other prominent local businesspeople. Everyone was wearing black and white, even to the jewelry the ladies wore. At

the center of the table was a white Christmas tree, decked with black ornaments.

"*Black* Christmas tree ornaments?" the ghost asked.

"The senator's wife is radically chic, I hear," Monica told him.

With all the talk of tightening the budget that was going on in government, the senator had spared no expense. Waiters clad in tuxes with tails and holly sprig boutonnieres delivered not only goose and turkey and succulent honey-roasted ham, but all sorts of other beautifully prepared dishes to the table. At a side table, a bartender made drinks to order. The bar had its own centerpiece: an ice sculpture of the manger scene at Bethlehem.

"The Lord driving the moneychangers from the temple would have been more appropriate," said the ghost.

"These are my friends!" Monica said.

"Listen to them then."

"Lovely decorations, Julia," someone was complimenting Mrs. Johansen. "The grounds are particularly impressive."

"Aren't they? You can thank Mr. Priestly," she said, nodding at a youngish, red-haired man who looked as if he worked out regularly.

"It was nothing," he said. "Bob won us the right to log a bit of woodland in a former Boy Scout camp. Of course, the spotted owl people raised their usual fuss, but finally we have some good heads in the Capitol building, and the tree huggers got nowhere. Once the trees were down, you know, I thought, what with the time of year and all, it was a shame to cut them up right away. They're very valuable, of course, but so's good legal help. I knew Bob and Julia were having this shindig before their trip to Hong Kong where they'll have their real Christmas when the rest of us are vacuuming tinsel off the carpet and putting the tree in the wood chipper. So I thought as a little Christmas bonus, we could take some of those trees and spruce them up—heh heh—and transplant them before we send them off to Japan. Very expensive operation, of course, but I spare no expense when it comes to my friends at Christmas."

"That's nice," Monica said. The spirit said nothing but nodded to the opposite end of the table, where the senator, who was aglow with holiday spirit himself, was talking about the days before he came into political power and the job he had worked as a reclamation agent for a credit firm. He and Monica had discussed the work in the past. She felt in many ways that was why they were friends. Her work for the IRS had involved dealing with the same whining, the same pleading, the same lies and excuses, and the same need to be firm. Of course, the senator's work was more exciting than that, as he was explaining to his guests.

"Thing is," the senator was saying, "nobody thinks anybody else is working on Christmas day. People who've hidden a car at a friend's house will come and get it to take it for a spin, or people will go visiting relatives and leave their houses unguarded. That's when we'd go take back the furniture or take the car out of the driveway."

"This guy was the best!" said one of the senator's law partners. "I don't think anything ever got away from him. Once there were these deadbeats that claimed they couldn't pay for their truck 'cause the wife had a heart attack and was in ICU. We look and look and can't find it. Go to the guy's house about a jillion times, check every hospital in the city. Finally, Christmas day, we find it in the staff parking lot at Virginia Mason. Guy claimed he'd sold it to send us the payment, but I dunno."

"What happened to the wife?"

"Who cares?" the senator's admirer said. "They were deadbeats, right, Bob? Hadn't been for deadbeats like them, we'd never have made it through law school."

"I thought your father owned Yachtsman's National Bank, Bob," the owner of another bank said.

"He does, but I worked for everything I have, the same way he did," Johansen said. "It's the American way."

"Didn't wait to inherit it, like the Banks woman, eh?" said one of the congressmen who had been responsible for some of the antitrust suits against Databanks.

Turning to the Ghost of Christmas Present, she said, "I'm surprised Bob even lets that man in his house. But I suppose if he's going to negotiate with him, he has to talk to him."

The Spirit of Christmas Present, for all his flesh now looked remarkably like Scrooge, the former money lender, as he raised a cynical eyebrow and nodded toward Senator Johansen.

"A fool and her money are soon parted, Freddie," said Johansen who was full of his own spirits and in an expansive mood. "Poor little Money is headed for a fall. The suits you've brought have slowed down Databanks enough for the competition to come close. When Monica brings out our program, once the public and the press find out that Data-banks has helped add a sort of federal patrol to the infor-mation highway, the consumers are going to be peeved with Databanks."

"Her stock will go down," Freddie said. "She might even have to sell out. And there will be lots of mutual friends of ours—"

Bob Johansen put his finger to his lips. "Please, Freddie, Christmas is a time for keeping secrets. We wouldn't want to be accused of trying to predict opportunities for insider trading, would we?"

Freddie shut up.

"Let's get out of here," Monica said. "I thought you were supposed to make me *like* Christmas. What a snake. I'll show *him* who the public is going to hate."

"Christmas is not the time for hatred," the Ghost of Christmas Present said with a pious voice and a wolfish smile.

She stepped toward the door, but as she did, someone from the dining room yelled, "Hey!" and Monica jumped before she realized she couldn't be seen.

"Hello there," the ghost said, looking down. Monica fol-lowed his gaze. A dainty, fluffy cat with beautiful calico markings sat on her haunches before him, her front paws raised to snatch the hem of his robe. She was meowing like crazy.

From the dining room, Mrs. Johansen, she of the blond highlights and the hard eyebrows, called, "Oh, dear, it's Chanel. Jefferson, would you please collect her and return her to the kitchen until the soiree is over?" She turned to her guests and said, "She used to be such a mellow creature, but then she went into heat and got out one night and threw kittens whose father obviously wasn't her calibre. We had to get rid of them of course—"

The cat squawled as one of the tuxedoed men scooped her up.

"Don't worry. I won't forget," the ghost said, and he and Monica were once more in the sleigh.

"What was that all about?" Monica asked. "I thought we couldn't be seen by anyone there? Or are you going to tell me that was a ghost cat?"

"Oh, no, she was alive, though heartbroken, poor thing. Don't look at me that way. I certainly didn't expect such an incident, but there was something peculiar about that animal. Or perhaps it is so with all animals, that they are not troubled by the boundaries between life and death as humans are. We were there and the cat knew we were there, and furthermore knew that, unlike living souls, I might understand her appeal."

"Great, fine, very touching. So where are we now?"

"Why, you wanted to visit friends, so I thought we could visit another friend of yours. Don't you recognize this place?"

It was a large, rambling house in the suburbs. No lights were lit but a rather cheerless swag of greenery with a couple of pinecones wired to it was hooked to the front door.

"No."

The spirit led her straight through the door and she saw

Wayne, wearing an overcoat, sitting in the cold with a phone in his hand. "I can't make it, Ma. Sea-Tac is closed for the storm, and nothing's leaving Boeing Field, either. No, Ma, you're not in Seattle anymore. You're in Florida, remember? Where it's warm." A pause. Wayne ran his hand over his face. He no longer looked boyish.

Visions of that first Christmas with the Reillys were still fresh in Monica's mind as she heard Wayne say to Mrs. Reilly, who had given her the lace collar and who was the baker of the best bread she'd ever tasted, "Let me talk to the nurse again, Ma. Ma? Yes, the one you call Moira, after Aunt Mary's girl. No, she's not, she's—just hand the phone to her, okay, Ma? No, I'm not mad at you, Mammy. No, darlin', of course I'm not. I love you, and I'll get there as soon as I can. Merry Christmas."

Another pause then, "Oh, hi, Meredith, how are you doing? Having a good holiday? I know. It's hard. I'm sorry, but having you there made me feel better. I can't make it to-night at least. Airport's closed. I'll be out there as soon as this clears up, but we're socked in. Look, anything she wants, okay? Just bill me. I've arranged for a few things to come out there for her and the others and a bit of appreciation for yourselves. Kiss her for me and tell her . . . you know. Merry Christmas."

He hung up, shoved his glasses up to wipe his eyes, and looked around the living room of his decorator-furnished house, full of polished steel and Chihuly glass that had absolutely no connection with the Wayne that Monica knew. She was pretty sure he'd taken the stuff in trade for services at some time or the other. He still lived in the nineteenth century in a lot of ways, a strange quirk for a techie.

Then he showed his true stripes by stalking out of the living room and into a den full of books: not decorator bound ones but paperback technical trade books in piles around a computer station, and floor-to-ceiling shelves full of Mark Twain, Robert Louis Stevenson, Kipling, Sir Walter Scott, and O. Henry in one section. In another area were the complete Star Wars and Star Trek series, plus many science fiction and fantasy authors: Greg Bear, Megan Lindholm, Vonda N. McIntyre, Don McQuinn, William Deitz, Bill Ransom, Elizabeth Ann Scarborough, Jack Cady, Terry Brooks, Rod Garcia y Robertson, Sara Stamey, Amy Thompson, Ursula K. LeGuin, Kristine Katherine Rusch, Nina Kirriki Hoffman, Dean Wesley Smith, Jerry Oltion, Damon Knight, Spider Robinson, Bill Gibson, Michael Coney, Kate Wilhelm, and John Dalmas—all Pacific Northwest writers.

Monica looked inside the books, not by touching them, just by looking. They were all signed, and at least one per author was signed to Wayne with gratitude for sorting out some software problem or the other. She remembered he had run a consulting business on the side for many years. The shelves ran on to other science fiction by people whose names were vaguely familiar to Monica: Asimov, McCaffrey, Silverberg, Beagle, Norton, Pratchett, and many others, shoved in wherever he'd found a spot when he finished reading the book. None of them were fancy and all looked well-worn.

There were mysteries, too. Again, Pacific Northwest authors were in one section: J. A. Jance, Earl Emerson, Candace Robb, K. K. Beck, Ann Rule, Sharon Newman, and Mary Daheim—more than she had thought possible. Classic mysteries occupied another section: Christie, Hammet, and so forth. Other favorite authors were in yet another section. Her eye lit on the M's and P's: McCleod, McCrumb, Michaels, Perry, Peters, and Pickard.

Separating the spaces was an empty fireplace made of stone, not steel. The floor was wood, with Navajo rugs scattered around. There was an Easyboy chair, a wildly expensive office chair like the one Monica had (she suspected either he gave himself and Doug matching ones or the other way around), and a gigantic computer station. A stained glass lamp hung overhead, and beside the desk was an empty box with a flannel-cased pillow covered in cat fur. She remembered hearing that Doug's only pet, a yellow cat named Bozobit, had recently died. She remembered quite a bit about Wayne, now that she thought about it. She'd been paying more attention than she realized.

The place was not littered, dusty, or dirty, which made Monica think he probably had help in to clean. The swag on the door was the only hint of Christmas, though, which was sad. Wayne had always loved Christmas. But then, he'd been counting on spending it with his mother. It was sad that he'd ended up alone in his empty house without even his cat.

But the companionship he had now was where he'd usually found it—inside his computer. He had left it on with

a Star Trek screen saver running—the new edition, with
Chakotay calling on his animal spirits to save the ship.

"Won't we be on there?" Monica asked. "How wide does
this haunting spread, anyway?"

The Ghost of Christmas Present shook his head, put his
finger to his lips, and pointed.

Wayne called for his E-mail. The screen scrolled down and
down and down so that Monica could imagine it stretching
page after page across the room if it was hard copy.

He clicked on the first message, and clicked "Read."

With a swoosh and snap that blew Monica's hair straight
back, she and the spirit found themselves in a high school
gymnasium lined with sleeping bags and filled with all sorts
of people in rugged clothes, rubber boots, sweaters, coats,
and slickers. In the center of the room was a Christmas tree
and beneath it were wrapped packages, open boxes of
smoked meats, fruits, nuts, and sweets from mail-order food
firms and Seattle caterers. Children were playing with
mostly waterproof toys except for the ones that were playing
with the wrapping. Sitting in a corner, with his back
propped up against a blanket roll, a young man sat tapping
on a notebook computer. A cord snaked across the floor and
over through an open door to an office telephone. "Dear
Paddy," the man wrote, as Monica could tell because she
could look right over his shoulder. "This is not exactly a
traditional Christmas. The floods have wiped out a good
portion of the Skagit Valley, though the sandbags and crews
of neighbors saved Mount Vernon. I'm getting ready to go
out with one of the rowboat crews Search and Rescue and

the Humane Society are organizing to look for people and animals trapped by the flood. Just wanted you to know this is one of the craziest Christmases I've ever seen. Some anonymous donor sent a big tree to the shelter, complete with presents and tons of food for the victims and volunteers. Also, the insurance companies have already been sending agents around to assess damage and some checks have been cut already. Someone has definitely applied pressure someplace. Maybe it was that E-mail message I wrote bawling out Johansen, you figure? Thanks for your words of concern, Paddy, but Janet and the kids are fine. The kids were scared at first, but now I think they're high on the adrenaline and thrilled by the novelty, though a little worried about Patches, our dog. Gotta go catch a rowboat and try to find the critter. Happy Holidays, Ralph."

Monica and the spirit swooshed again and found themselves back in Wayne's den. He was smiling a little as he read the letter.

"He's Paddy, right?" she asked the spirit. "He sent all those things and put the screws to the insurance companies? Either that, or he's already monitoring other peoples' E-mail and we're behind the times with Get a Life. But you'd think I'd have heard about it."

"Oh, really!" the spirit said, sounding exasperated with her turn of mind.

Wayne clicked on another E-mail message and they were transported to a hospital. The scene was not cheerful. "Sarajevo, day four of the new cease-fire," a woman journalist typed. She wrote of the day she'd spent watching the few doctors and nurses try to care for injured people, of how little food there was, and how much despair in the wake of an ugly, debilitating war.

Monica read what the woman was writing but paid only the scantest attention to it, really. She was wandering like the ghost she resembled among corpselike infants tied to cribs, hollow-eyed women and girls with arms the size of chopsticks and faces so emaciated you could count the teeth in their closed mouths sticking out, screaming old people missing limbs or with head injuries. The place was filthy and the doctors and nurses couldn't even wash their hands, much less the ward.

"Get us out of here," she said to the spirit.

The spirit himself was dismayed. Never had he beheld a less Christmassy place, even in the slums of his own London.

Then she noticed a GI standing at the entrance to the ward. He was not young and looked like he might have been a bank clerk or a real estate broker at home, which was entirely possible since many of the troops were from reserve units. A nurse looked up, furtively, afraid he'd take up her time.

"Ma'am, some of the children at home heard about the babies here and how they just lie tied in bed all day with nothing to look at and—well, I know it isn't much, but some of us who have kids or used to be teachers got classes to make origami figures. We got 'em strung into mobiles for the babies. Be glad to hang them. Promise not to get in your way."

The nurse nodded and waved at him and he motioned for a couple of younger men, both agile and tall, to follow.

They brought with them sacks of paper birds and boxes, strung with olive drab thread, and tacked or taped or tied them to the bars above the various cribs. The other children on the ward watched warily, as if expecting the figures to explode, and very slowly, some of the young ones tied to the beds began to follow the mobiles with their eyes. It wasn't Christmas, no one actually smiled, but maybe it was a little less bleak.

The older man started to leave and the nurse said, "Wait. Could we have that tape? The extra thread? Have you any tacks left?"

He gave them to her and then she did smile. "Thank you and—thank the children for us. It looks nicer."

She turned back to bandage a stump.

Monica and the spirit were once more in Wayne's den. His head was in his hands as he read the letter from the journalist. He clicked on another.

They were on the Pacific Coast of the Olympic Penninsula. Monica recognized it from family vacations when she and Doug were children. But the town they were in was run-down, weatherbeaten, water-stained, the sky full of lashing rain and sleet, the sea tossing restlessly in its sleep, vomiting mare's tails up over the highway and the flimsy looking buildings. Houses here were mobile homes, most of them old, with thrown-together wanagins attached and weed-strewn, junk-clogged yards. In one of these a man wrote, "Paddy, as you know, the fishing for the Makah people was not good this year. And while some of us may be happy for the sake of the trees that the timber industry isn't doing too hot, it's bad news for the families here supported by logging. With the BIA cutbacks, the clinic had to close and we may have only one teacher next year. The Food Bank brought stuff to help a lot of families, but some of it sure is weird. Who wants the artichoke hearts and hoisin sauce on their canned beans, I wonder?"

This man wasn't the only one in the trailer. Bodies slept everywhere. There had to be twenty people in there. And there was a wood stove blazing away, but Monica could see it barely heated a space two feet away from itself because it leaked most of the heat up the chimney. The wind blew through the cracks, and the man writing the message shivered. "He has money enough for a computer, I see," she said, "for all his complaining."

"Probably that's what they spent all their money on," the ghost said. "Computers and other elaborate equipment. Let's look." But they found very little else in the way of technical equipment or luxuries in any of the private homes, except for televisions, many of which were broken or had such bad reception as to be useless. Across kitchen tables and on sofas lay many beautiful pieces of artwork, however: carving, basketry, and beadwork in progress and hidden away in packages in many of the homes, waiting for the families to wake up.

Monica felt dizzy with all the traveling they did that night, visiting the people in Wayne's computer. Not all of it was sad. The music interest newsgroups were full of parties among friends, some of the people in the book discussion groups got new books or the loan of new books from others in their group, but usually, at the other end of the click, someone was sitting alone, typing a message to someone else they'd never met. Intellectual messages, political messages, lovelorn messages, hysterical messages, angry messages, sleazy messages, crazy messages, business messages, humorous messages, and merely chatty messages. Wayne didn't read them all. He chose only some, and most of them he answered as Paddy, but he sent kind words, funny words, soothing words, encouraging words, and stern words to many, and to a few he sent a bit more than that. Monica had never seen this side of him, and she realized how little she knew of him. Well, how could anyone have known either him or Doug, unless they were available through a computer? But she was pretty sure Doug's communication never went like this. There was a lot of the kind and generous boy she had met when his mother made her that first good Christmas after the death of her parents.

"There!" she said to the ghost. "That one's scamming, plain as day. And there's that married guy, trying to con girls."

"And there's the class of deaf youngsters wishing merry Christmas to their hearing friends, and there's the young mother, who has to stay at home with her sick baby but has no funding, borrowing her friend's computer to ask for advice about her baby's illness. If it was in an orphanage, where it belongs, she wouldn't have to annoy her friend with her demands."

"I get the point," Monica said, hearing her own opinions mimicked back to her.

"Oh, and there's one who's being hounded by the tax collectors for debts incurred by her dead husband, who of course neglected to tell her about them. What sort of person would hound that poor widow at Christmas, do you suppose? Why, it would take someone as mean as I once was—"

"Oh, shut up," Monica said, but she got the point.

She wouldn't have been surprised if some of the people they met weren't people she'd dunned when she was working for the government. It seemed to her they met most of the United States, half of Canada, and a good portion of the world that night over the Internet. People who owned computers, people who went to work before and after hours to use business computers, people who borrowed computers from friends or rented them at copy shops and cafés, open on Christmas specifically for their user customers. Many were lonely or desperate or desperate to help desperate people they knew. And through their computers many other people responded. There was nothing subversive about most of the groups, but she would not have been surprised to know that Senator Johansen would have been interested in the contents of their files.

Wayne was staring thoughtfully at the screen when they rejoined him in his den, and he punched a couple of keys too rapidly for Monica to see what he did, but neither she nor the ghost departed with those keystrokes.

Then he hit one more and they found themselves alone in a darkened building of concrete and wire and smelling of antiseptic, used kitty litter, and wet dog. In an office, accompanied by a brindled guardian cat of considerable fluff and importance, a woman sat typing into a Macintosh: "Dear Paddy, I couldn't bear to think of the critters alone on Christmas Eve so I came back in to keep them company for awhile. Very few people adopted pets for Christmas this year, and we had more strays than usual dumped on us. One little puppy—purebred lab from the look of him—was dumped in the fenced yard of a woman who doesn't like dogs. Another little dog was found in the parking lot at Boeing. And I came to work a week ago to find a whole litter of kittens freezing their pencil-stub tails off in front of the door. They looked like poster kids for the Humane Society, they're so cute, fluffy, and wide-eyed. At least they were mostly weaned and only needed a little more bottle feeding. But we can't keep them too much longer."

Monica turned to see the Ghost of Christmas Present dangling a piece of yarn for a fluffy, blue-eyed kitten in a cage to bat at. Two of its siblings dozed, but two were sitting up, one yawning, one ready to jump in.

"What is this? I'm getting guilt-tripped for Christmas? Wayne must be losing it to be spending the night this way! Why doesn't he just go back to work or something?" she complained, but her whining fell on deaf ears as the spirit was busy laughing at the kitten doing backward somersaults to catch the yarn between its pink paw pads.

Another click and they were watching as Wayne sighed and shrugged his shoulders and looked mournfully at the empty cat bed.

"Spirit, just let me out of this—whatever it is, and I promise, I'll go straight to that shelter when I wake up and get

Wayne a cat. Hell, it's a big house. I'll get him the whole damned litter. But—"

The spirit shook his head and pointed. Wayne was reading another message. Monica and the spirit read over his shoulder. He was picking up a message to him from a group called Soulmates. "Aha," Monica said. "Wayne's been courting?"

But though the message was from a woman, the tone wasn't what Monica expected.

"Hi, Paddy," the message said. "Sorry to hear it's such a bummer for you. Sorry you couldn't make your girl see reason. You sound like a nice guy. You say you grew up with her younger brother and you think she still thinks of you that way even though you're both in your forties. That's a toughie. Maybe it's not really that. Sometimes, by the time a person has reached middle age, they've just been hurt so many times they make up reasons not to respond to someone who might care for them. She sounds lonely, from what you say. Please be careful and don't get caught up in that thing a lot of nice guys do—my husband did before he met me— of finding some total witch to romanticize about and believing she really has a heart of gold. If you hadn't told me how selfless this woman had been raising your friend after their parents died, I'd be ready to put her in the cold and heartless category. Anyway, I hope it works out for you, Wayne. Merry Christmas. LauraH@ranier.com."

The spirit beamed at Monica, who sputtered, "I never, I—What's he doing, writing about me? I—he's just a kid—"

"He looks grown-up enough to me, actually," the spirit said. "But obviously he's wasting his time on a woman too preoccupied to see his worth. Shall we go, my dear? There's still much to do—"

"I have done more visiting tonight than I've ever done in all my life put together, I think," she said. "I give up. Uncle. You sold me. Christmas is good. I am lucky. Many are not. I should give more. And, whatever that bastard Johansen wants, he is definitely not getting it from me, no matter what. Those people writing to Wayne deserve their privacy and—"

"As to that, I think I really must in all fairness show you something," he said. Fortunately, Wayne used a glide-point mouse device, which was quite easily ghost manipulated. The cursor arrived at the icon bearing the Databanks avatar, a vault with a question mark, and clicked.

Monica caught a glimpse of Wayne's startled face before she and the ghost were swooshing once more to end up back at Databanks. Not in her office but staring out through multiple screens at her staff. The staff she was paying to be working the holiday developing Johansen's software. Instead, they were all watching her like she was some sort of soap opera.

"What is this?" she demanded of the ghost.

"Why, it's your employees, obviously," the ghost said, clearly waffling.

"I know that. Why can I see them? Can they see me?"

"Oh, yes. A greeting might be in order, in fact. Might I suggest 'Merry Christmas?' "

"Hi, Ms. Banks! You sure look natural!" Phillip said, as if of a well-made-up corpse.

"Look at that color resolution. I never knew your eyes were so blue, Ms. Banks," Dave said admiringly.

"Spirit, you look terrific," Melody said. "I keep wanting to tell you what I want for Christmas."

"A new job would be appropriate," Monica said.

"Oops. Backsliding, eh?" Sheryl said, shaking her head. "Ms. Banks, you've already fired most of us if we don't have Get a Life ready by New Year's and, with you and your spooky friends taking up all our on-line time, I don't think we're going to."

"Now look at the color resolution!" Dave said even more admiringly. "That shade of red you're turning matches the spirit's robe exactly, Ms. Banks."

"Don't just sit there, you two," Melody said sweetly. "I know you have lots more to accomplish. Never mind us. We're seeing a side of you we never knew existed, boss."

"Yeah," Harald said. "Pardon my sexism but, gee, Monica, you know you're really cute when you're *not* angry."

"Mutiny, that's what this is," Monica said to the spirit.

"You're not a ship's captain, Money," John told her. "You're the president of a company whose function you don't understand, whose staff you resent, and whose resources you're putting to improper use."

"Not only that," Miriam said, "we're not sailors. We're subcontractors and will probably go on to form competing companies."

"That is, unless you find some way to make it worth our while to stay," Sheryl said.

"I don't think this is exactly the spirit of Christmas, ladies and gentlemen," the spirit said. "No business to be transacted on the holiday. Thank you very much. Miss Banks and I have another stop to make. Merry Christmas to you all."

"And to all a gooooood night," Sheryl said, and she had the gall to sneer.

Twelve

∽

This time the spirit and Monica reappeared in the horse-drawn sleigh instead of inside Wayne's office.

"Why is it that we're not swooshing this time?" Monica asked.

"All of those visits were paid to people who were on-line. The visit we're making now is to someone who is not—at least, not ordinarily. Besides, it gives us a chance to take a more scenic route."

Monica was rather hoping they'd go back through the forest again, but instead, they drove through the downtown district of Seattle and down to the southern end. On several occasions, when gangs were celebrating Christmas in their own special way, Monica had cause to be glad that they were invisible, at least to everyone but cats.

They stopped at the end of a block, by a bus stop, and dismounted. "What?" she asked the ghost. The snow was falling only very lightly now and the streets looked like glass. "Are we going too far for a ghostly sleigh or are the horses tired? Is that why we're taking the bus?"

"We're not taking it, we're meeting it," the Spirit of Christmas Present said.

"You don't think that's carrying season's greetings a little far?" she asked. She wasn't cold anymore, and the wind had died down, but she wanted to be back on her own couch in her own office. She was wearying of revelations and feared more of them.

He laughed with annoying merriment at her sarcasm, as if it was amusing. A bus pulled up and disgorged a few late-night stragglers. Most of them were drunk. One was a woman in boots, fishnet stockings, and a black leather jacket longer than her skirt. Behind her, a man carried a little girl, not because she was sleeping. She was wide awake and laughing at something someone had said. Then she looked around her and stopped laughing. "It's not snowing any-more," she said, as if someone had snatched a present.

"What do you care?" the fishnet stockinged woman asked her tiredly. "It's not like you could build snowmen or any-thing, and if you could, they'd get stolen by morning, don't ask me what for."

"Long night, Tiffany?" the man asked.

"I know him!" Monica said to the ghost. "That's the guy who cleans at night—one of them, anyway. Whassisname? Moses?"

"Noah," the ghost said.

"Who's the chippie? His wife?"

"Give Tina to me, Daddy," the woman said. "She's not heavy."

"I could walk if you'd brought my crutches, Grandad," the little girl said.

"It's too icy, baby," the man said. "We got by okay, didn't we? You and me goin' to pick your mama up so she didn't have to come home from her work alone on Christmas?"

"Thanks, Daddy," the woman said. "Only the lonely—and the total bizarros—are out right now. Not that a guy your age carrying a kid is a lot of protection."

"No, but we're company," he said. "Aren't we, Tina?"

She grinned and nodded, and Monica and the ghost followed them up many flights of stairs. Several of the individual steps were in bad need of repair. The woman and man knew the hazards well, however, and avoided them without hesitation. The building smelled of mildew and rotten wood, urine and mouse droppings, smoke and booze, sweat and burned TV dinners.

Noah's hard-faced daughter opened the door to their apartment. It was dark. "Jamie! Brianna!" Tiffany called.

"Come out, come out, wherever you are!" Tina caroled and suddenly the lights went on and there, suspended from the central lightbulb, was a Christmas tree of sorts, its proud creators looking on. It was made of used aluminum foil, taped and bent into a cone and cut so that pieces could be extended to form fronds from which tiny bits of colored plastic paper shone in the white light of the formerly bare bulb.

"It's beautiful!" Tina exclaimed.

"Look at that," Monica said to the ghost. "My guess

would have been that they'd have been out dealing drugs while the old man and the woman were gone."

"You see, my dear Monica, being wrong can sometimes be a pleasure," the ghost replied.

Then she looked at the dinner Noah had prepared before going to fetch his daughter.

"Tuna casserole for Christmas dinner?" she asked the ghost. "What happened to the basket with the ham in it, that kind of thing? Don't poor people always get free food at Christmas?"

"Of course, of course, my dear. But these are gainfully employed people. Surely that man makes enough at your place of business that, coupled with his daughter's pay where she—er—plies her trade, they could afford a sumptuous meal."

"Yeah. Of course they can. I think. Actually, they're subcontractors, too. I'm not sure what they make. Probably he drinks. Or gambles. What I can't figure out is why are they acting so *happy* when they're miserably, putridly poor."

"Maybe because they help each other. Maybe because there's love in this house holding them together," the spirit said.

"You are Victorian, aren't you?" Monica said, meaning to mock, but ending up merely smiling before she resumed watching the family as they cleared the table that had served as a study desk and sculpture studio for one of the kids whose medium seemed to be Popsicle sticks. They set the table under the supervision of Brianna while Jamie pulled the casserole out of the oven and Tina's mother went into another room to change her clothes, returning in jeans and a sweatshirt, her face washed and her hair pulled back in a ponytail that made her look very young.

When the table was laid, they sat on a variety of things around it, including a portable TV that seemed to have been broken for some time. The little redheaded girl with the crippled legs and the grandfather were the only ones who actually had a chair. The mother and Brianna sat on two plastic trunks piled together, and the boy, Jamie, on a footstool. Noah had a seat-sprung easy chair and the little girl took the straight-backed chair.

"Okay, time to say the blessing," Brianna said. Monica thought the way she had been stage-managing everyone and bossing her brother amusing. "You start, Grandpa."

"Okay, I'm grateful that Ms. Banks didn't catch Tina under the desk this morning."

Tina giggled. "And I'm grateful she didn't catch Doug and me before we were finished."

That stopped the blessings right there. Tiffany turned to her daughter and demanded, "Doug who? Who is this Doug? Daddy, you were watching my baby, weren't you? You wouldn't let any strange Doug—"

"Calm down now, honey. Nothing to get upset about. Doug is just Tina's imaginary friend she made up when she started coming to work with me. Isn't that right, Tina?"

Tina scrunched up one side of her face and appeared to be thinking about that. "Sorta," she said finally.

"Sorta what?" her mother demanded.

"Well, he's sorta real and sorta not. He's not like, in person, he's over the computer. Except I think I saw his face once."

"Computer?" Noah's voice was ominously quiet. "What computer, Tina? You know you weren't supposed to touch them. If I got fired—"

"And he *will*," Monica said, feeling tricked. She had started to think that here was at least one hardworking employee whose work she could understand, whose problems she could sympathize with, only to find out he'd been tricking her like everyone else who worked for her.

"The one in the office," Tina said. "And it's okay, Grandpa. Doug was the owner before your Miss Banks. She's his sister. He wanted me to help him make her a Christmas present." She chewed her lip some more. "Sorta. It's pretty complicated, Grandpa."

"He was there with you working on the computer?" Her mother's knuckles were white on the table. "And you didn't tell Grandpa?"

"No, Mama. He wasn't with the computer. He was *in* it. Mostly, he just wrote me notes, but once I think I saw him."

Noah was shaking his head at his daughter. "Nobody was there with her, Tiffany. I was watching. I couldn't listen though, because of the machines. You mean to tell me that whole time you were in there you were playing with the computer, Tina? Even though I told you not to?"

"Yes, but it was a secret, Grandpa, and Doug said I couldn't tell anyone, even you. Except, now that it's Christmas Eve, she's probably got her present already so it's okay. I hope she likes it."

"What is it, honey?" Brianna asked more maternally than either of the adults.

Tina shrugged. "Some kinda game. Doug was going to introduce her to Ebenezer Scrooge, from the book, so she wouldn't be lonely and mean anymore. But there was this game first, and someone called the Program Manager who wrote stuff that looked like it was in the Bible. Grandpa, I think he was God. I think Doug is an angel, so it's okay, you won't lose your job."

"Hah!" Monica scoffed, so loudly that it seemed as if, when a mighty gust of wind bowed the window in and outside the transformers popped in a brilliant flash of light and the power went out, Monica was somehow responsible. She paid no attention whatsoever to the dramatic change in weather, which was accompanied by more heavy gusts splatting clumpy, wet snowflakes against the window.

As one voice, the people in the tiny apartment stood up and cheered and ran to the window to look out at the fireworks created by the popping transformers.

"Turn on the radio, Jamie. I bet the news people are having a good time with this storm," Noah said.

But all of that went unnoticed by Monica, who was good and angry at what she had been forced to endure at the hands of children, literary devices, gamesters, cleaning men, dead brothers, and possibly a Program Manager who might or might not have been God. She said as much to the spirit, ending by saying, ". . . and furthermore, I want to go back to my office right now, Spirit. I know where this is in your little plan. I'm supposed to get all mushy over the differently abled little dolly and turn into Lady Bountiful. Well, forget it. The brat has been playing with valuable equipment and conspiring against me with my sanctimonious sibling, who hasn't been the least improved by death as near as I can tell. I want to go back to my nice, comfy couch, and I will forget you and everything tonight and take a Gaviscon and it will all be better."

The spirit, she saw to her satisfaction, was extremely dismayed. "You would have made an admirable matron in a workhouse," he told her. "You are made of very stern stuff indeed. I'm afraid you're lost, despite all our efforts. So, very well, we'll return."

But when they tried to leave the room, they found they couldn't move beyond the walls that confined them. They could not use the door, they could not swoosh, they could not wish themselves back to the sleigh or to Monica's office. They remained within the darkened interior where the children crowded at the window watching the snow fall, the wind blow, and the power lines undulate in their shocking dances, while Tiffany and Noah lit candles and the people on the newscasts invited listeners from around the Sound to call in and tell how the storm was ruining their Christmas.

At one such story, Jamie looked back approvingly at the radio. "Wow! The whole roof of their house blew off! Cool!"

"Yeah, of course it was, nerd-brain," his sister brushed the top of his head with her fist. "Freezing."

"I like it when they have this kinda broadcast," Tiffany said. "Makes you feel like everyone in the area is like in one little town, y'know? It would be better on TV, though, where you could see."

"No it wouldn't, Mama," Tina said. "If it were TV, it wouldn't work now 'cause the power's out."

"That's it, of course," Monica said, slapping her head. "God, here I was getting all panicky and there's a simple explanation. This whole thing is an elaborate, maybe, okay, I'll give you, *maybe* supernaturally enhanced computer game. And the power's off. Somehow that cuts us off, too. We just have to stay till it comes back on." She nudged the Spirit of Christmas Present. "Didn't think of that one, did you?"

"My dear lady, I'm from an earlier time than this one. Electricity wasn't—"

"Yeah, yeah, excuses, excuses. It didn't take a genius to figure it out, just a little clear-headed thinking, none of this sentimental stuff you and Doug are throwing at me. Hah!"

"Grandad, can we go out and play in the snow now?" Tina asked.

"Not in this wind and with all the sparks flying. Maybe in the morning, if it's still there. I think right now Brianna and Jamie should clean off the table, we'll put the candles there and play Skipbo, okay?"

"I'll get the cards, Dad," Tina's mother said.

Monica had planned to stay aloof and bored during the card game, but the room was very small and the little circle cast by the candle made it cozy. She could hardly sleep in her incorporeal form and there was nowhere to sit. And the Ghost of Christmas Present got busy immediately kibbitzing with everybody's hand.

"Hey, I thought you were here to show me something," she complained.

"I tried," the spirit said. "But you quit, remember? Still, no reason to ruin a perfectly good Christmas. That's it, Tina girl. You've got him. He's got nothing to play on that and you're going to go out!" The spirit seemed to have grasped the rules of contemporary card games very quickly.

"You're cheating!" Monica complained. "You're favoring the little girl just because she looks like she belongs on a tele-thon."

"Am not," the spirit said.

"Are too," Monica insisted.

"Am *not*," the spirit insisted harder. "And if you think I am, then you ought to get over here and help some of the others instead of pouting."

"I'm not pouting."

"Are too."

"Am not. Oh, for pity's sake, anything to shut you up. First it was cats singing Christmas carols, now this."

She hadn't played cards since she was a child, and it took her longer than it had taken the spirit to learn the game, but once she did, she and the rest of the table took on the spirit and Tina.

Jamie made large, swaggering gestures as he laid down his cards. Tiffany, who'd wanted to go to college to study psychology, assessed the latent hostility or envy or feelings of deprivation behind each move of her opponents. Brianna tried to tell everyone else what to do. Noah pulled Jamie's baseball cap low on his forehead, like an eyeshade, tried hard to look sneaky, and several times made rather obvious and ridiculous moves just to hear the kids holler that he was cheating.

Tina whined. "That's not *fair*. I wasn't *ready*. You didn't give me any good *cards*." And then she beat everybody else. Every single hand.

"Well," said Noah, four hands later, rising to his feet. "I've had about enough of this. This is elder abuse, is what this is. I'm going to see if the phone's still working. There's a team over at Databanks who will have been up working all night. I'll call up and find out how things are going. Ms. Banks is up there in her little old apartment all by herself on Christmas Eve."

"Daddy, let those people check on her and take care of themselves. They make four times what you make, and I'm sure there's auxiliary power there, isn't there?"

"Well, sure, honey, but they're all real young people, and they don't necessarily know where to find the backups. Ms. Banks doesn't much trouble herself to find out about it. Used to be there was a crew on hand twenty-four hours a day, but she decided that was a waste of money. Penny-wise and pound-foolish, that girl. But anyhow, I'd better go call and see if everything's okay."

"What if it's not? Are you going to try to take a bus back out there tonight of all nights and leave your family for that stingy, dried-up old maid who would step over you if she saw you dying in the street?"

"Mama, that's not true!" Tina said suddenly, and so hotly that her mother paused in midsentence to stare at her. "Miss Banks does too care about other people. Doug told me she raised him from the time he was a little boy and worked all her Christmases to take care of him. They were orphans."

"Maybe so, but that doesn't make her care anything about anybody else. She wouldn't give a rat's ass if your little butt was kicked out on the street tomorrow. She's rich and she's mean and she's the enemy, Tina."

"If it wasn't for her, I wouldn't have a job, honey," Noah said. "And your job wouldn't be enough to keep us."

"Daddy, you're a fabricator, not a janitor! She could hire you to do what you're good at—"

"I'm trained in aircraft, not computers, Tiffany—"

"She could retrain you then! And pay you what you're worth. Then we could maybe start saving for Tina's surgery."

"Mama, she only just got her company. She doesn't know anybody. She's lonesome, and she's only mean because she's scared of everybody. I saw her when she talked to Grandpa, but she didn't see me. I think she needs some friends."

Tiffany, who had appeared very tough until then, melted suddenly, and tears formed in her eyes as she reached over and pulled her daughter's shoulders to her and kissed the top of her head. "Oh, angel girl. You just think that because you want friends and you can't get out and make them. You think everybody is as good as you are. But okay, we'll give ol' Money Banks the benefit of the doubt for your sake."

"I don't like her calling Tina 'angel,'" Monica told the spirit. "That sounds like she's not long for this world. She's crippled, but there's something else, isn't there?"

The spirit nodded toward Tina, who looked up at her mother, over at her grandfather, and to her aunt and uncle, who were proof that she had to be a pretty good kid, because they didn't even seem especially jealous of the attention she was getting. "Speaking of angels and that kinda stuff? I got something to tell all of you. You know the thing with my heart? Well, don't worry about it too much. See, I didn't tell you this, but Doug is—well, he's not exactly alive anymore. That's why Miss Banks has his company. He didn't exactly say he was an angel, but I could kinda tell. So anyway, if my heart stops working, I'll know somebody in the neighborhood so I won't be all alone."

"I don't want to hear about you going anywhere," Brianna said, putting her hands over her ears. "Just stop it."

"Bad move, Tina," Jamie said. "I've heard about kids meeting jerks on the Internet, people you definitely wouldn't want to be caught dead with. What if he's one of those?"

Noah began to say something when the lights came back on.

"Time to go," the spirit said.

"Wait a minute. I want to know what the score is with the kid. Her brother—"

"Uncle."

"Uncle then, is right. Doug is a jerk and absolutely no fit companion for that little girl to be stuck with. She'll be bored into oblivion. I thought her legs were screwed up and now there's this stuff about her heart. The kid likes me. You heard her. Who do I have to intimidate to get to the bottom of this?"

But the spirit was no longer with her. Instead, she found herself back on the couch, looking at her own reflection on the blank screen of her television.

Thirteen

"Oooh," Scrooge said, rubbing his hands. "I think that went rather well."

He had returned to one of the small offices and was addressing the Databanks employees. The young people were not at this time sitting near their separate monitors but shared one. The desk that normally contained reference books had been cleared and chairs dragged to it. Spread across its surface was a pack of cards with images of dragons and witches and the like on them.

"It was an E-ticket ride for sure. I forgot that in the story, Christmas Present was pleasant. I enjoyed it right up until the power went out. Then we had to submit to letting John beat us all at playing Magic," Miriam said. "What happened with Noah's family and Monica?"

"I think it went well," he said. "She was quite impressed with Tina. But she is a very difficult lady indeed, you know. *I* was quite in tears and already converted by the time the Ghost of Christmases to Come—er—came. Our dear Monica still feels that it is up to her to play Program Manager with the lives of others."

"Yeah, we noticed," Sheryl said. "You know, I hope if this turns her around, it's not going to be a case of—you know—trying to buy love, buy her way into goodness. Did that happen to you, Eb?"

"Er—I suppose so. Dunno, really, never thought about it. But I certainly, in retrospect, don't blame them if they cared more for me afterward than before. I tried to deserve their respect as well. Don't know what else one can do other than withhold, eh?"

"I guess not. But people really hate it if you give them things and then queen it over them," Sheryl said.

"Yes," Harald said. "Perhaps we should show her 'don't' videos of my mother."

"This really is quite difficult enough as it is, you know," Scrooge said. "I think I'd best conduct the program and let the Program Manager sort out the rest. I do think she was somewhat impressed by my impersonation of the Spirit of Christmas Present."

"Looks like it agreed with you, too, Eb," Dave said.

"Yeah, I was going to comment on that," Sheryl agreed. "No wattles, fewer lines around the eyes, rosier cheeks, brighter eyes—you sure you didn't take that extra time to have a face-lift?"

"Eh?" Scrooge asked, obviously confused.

"She's kidding," Phillip told him.

"But you do definitely look younger," Miriam told him. "You're not still morphing, are you? To a younger you, I mean?"

"Good heavens, no. I removed the morph at once, dear

lady, though I do feel that my time as the Spirit of Christmas Present quite invigorated me. I don't wonder that I look younger. I feel wonderful. But then, my last few Christmases have very much agreed with me, I find. Until I died, of course. That rather dampened things, so I'm quite happy to be enjoying another Yuletide."

"Well, yeah, as long as you get to control the whole thing it's nice enough, I guess," Sheryl said. "But if you'd been out there in the trenches—"

"Trenches?"

"The malls, the parking lots, the highways, and the various districts within the city, you'd probably be ready to say humbug to the whole thing again. Why do you think Wayne celebrates on-line?"

"I thought he was lonely—pining for Miss Banks."

"No way is that guy lonely. He's rich, generous, and nice as well. Everybody invites him every place. But he's also smart—and too nice to make somebody else do his Christmas shopping for him. So he watches the tube and goes out on the Net to play Santa. You don't catch him in the malls, though."

"Are these malls like the one we visited in our recent trip to Christmas in the past July?" Scrooge asked.

"Worse," everyone said in unison.

"We should show him," Melody said. "Otherwise, he's never going to understand why it's just not as easy for modern people to be as enthused about Christmas as Dickens."

"We can't," Dave pointed out. "It's past closing time."

"No, it's not," Curtis said with a grin, and held up a CD-ROM. "Not for The Mall That Wouldn't Close."

"That sounds more sinister than Marley ever appeared," Scrooge said. "What is it?"

"A joke gift a buddy of mine sent me. He videotaped the trip he and his wife made last year to the open-twenty-four-hours-a-day-during-the-holidays super mall to buy gifts for their kids. They went on a Saturday, which was the only day he had off. He turned it into a game on CD-ROM, interactive and updated to this year for the sick, sadistic thrill of sharing it with friends fortunate enough to be able to work through the holidays."

"It probably won't play with Scrooge still jamming the lines," John pointed out.

But the others urged Curtis to try, and he inserted the metallic disk in its little round bed and returned it to its berth within the computer. Nothing happened.

Then, above Scrooge's head, the Program Manager lit up in shining gilt letters and beneath it, a drop menu appeared, with the word *enter* illuminated by golden light.

Curtis looked around him and motioned to the others, who nodded, and everyone piled fingers atop the "Enter" key.

Immediately, Scrooge found himself horribly cramped in a small, enclosed space that seemed to be barreling along as if it were rolling down a mountainside. Beside him, Melody scruched sideways and on her other side, Curtis sat behind a platter-sized wheel. In back of him was the pressure of bodies piled upon bodies and the grunts, squeals, and giggles of the other young Databanks employees.

The most alarming thing was that all around them swarmed thousands upon thousands of red and white lights. Some flashed toward them like comets, some winked malevolently, all smeared with the constant downpour that was removed and replaced, removed and replaced, with the swiping of businesslike looking blades attached to the window through which he regarded the scene.

"Isn't this awesome?" Melody asked. "With Eb on board, Curtis's program went virtual."

"Way cool," someone else agreed.

But Sheryl said, "If I'd wanted to go Christmas shopping, I'd have done it by myself or with my sister, during the day, and I'd have picked my time. This is like a virtual nightmare. Anybody see the escape button?"

"Be brave, babe," Phillip told her in a grim, tight voice. "We seem to be in it for the duration."

"Where are we exactly?" Scrooge asked. "And are these hellish lights supposed to be decorative? I don't care for them at all."

"I-5 South," Curtis said, also grimly. "And no, the lights are for safety. Look closely and you'll see that the red ones are attached to the back end of cars—"

"Railroad cars?" Scrooge asked.

"Uh—horseless carriages, Eb," Miriam's voice said, and he felt a small hand giving him a reassuring pat on the shoulder.

"And the white lights are attached to the front end of the cars," Curtis finished.

"Then those are coming *toward* us?" Scrooge asked, feeling quite alarmed until he recalled that he was, in fact, already dead and so presumably a fatal collision could do him little harm. He wasn't sure what the effects would be on the young people, but although they didn't seem to be enjoying the ride much more than he did, they did appear to be rather used to it.

"In most places they're on a different road, going the other direction, with a big grass strip or trees or concrete—"

"Or a two-hundred-foot drop to oblivion below—" Phillip's voice interjected.

"Between them and us. We're pretty safe—"

The rest of her sentence was cut off as a pair of white lights overtook them from behind and Scrooge had the impression of tons of steel shooting past them like a charging elephant ridden by an enraged madman before it inserted itself in front of them, blinking its red lights at them. Suddenly, the entire conveyance containing Scrooge and his party slammed to a halt, squealing like a pig being roasted alive.

All around them similar sounds filled the air. Curtis uttered an oath.

"What is it?" Scrooge asked. "What's wrong?"

"Traffic jam ahead. Probably an accident like that butthead up in front almost caused us to have."

"Oh dear," Scrooge said. And then the lot of them waited tensely for what seemed like hours until finally their vehicle was allowed to creep along, encased on all sides by many other vehicles. Similar incidents occured no fewer than ten times until at last, when Scrooge inquired, "Another one?" Curtis answered, "Naw. Now we're just looking for a parking place."

"Ah," Scrooge said with satisfaction, thinking that with their arrival, their unpleasant interlude would soon be over.

However, after an hour and a half of playing tag with great long lines of cars, when Curtis pulled into a parking place and the vehicle breathed a sigh of relief to be divested of its human cargo, Scrooge was nearly knocked down by another car looking for its parking place. Or he would have been knocked down and possibly seriously injured had he not had the good fortune to be a ghost.

In the distance, within a vast field of vehicles as numerous and thickly massed as sand on the seashore, loomed an enormous building or series of buildings, many-tiered and many-doored. Scrooge could not tell if it was a factory or a castle, but he was assured by his companions that it was, in fact, the Mall.

"Keep together, people," Curtis said in the manner of a captain of the Royal Grenadiers. "We have no idea how this VR works. Mess up, and you could be Christmas shopping for all eternity."

By the brilliant white lights suspended over the field of vehicles and by the roaming lights of the parking-space-ravenous vehicles themselves, Scrooge saw his companions give a collective shudder.

The people in the parking lot reminded Scrooge a bit of London. People of every age and no doubt every occupation funneled through the doors, where each individual became another striving unit in the teeming mass of humanity jamming the aisles and hallways. Scrooge and his companions could scarcely see each other.

"Oh, look," Curtis said, pointing to a glowing rectangle in his hand. "A virtual shopping list."

"This just gets to be more fun by the minute, doesn't it?" Sheryl asked with patently false brightness.

"I think we'd better try to complete it, though," Curtis said. "This is a game, after all. I doubt we can leave until we're done. Either that or find the escape button again."

"Maybe we *should* split up—" Dave began.

"No way. Here's what we need." The list that followed was prodigious: "One God-Empress-of-the-Universe Barbie, spaceship for same, with carrying case that converts to launch pad for spaceship; women's medium blue robe and slippers, size nine; Nuke 'Em Playtime Plastique Explosive set with choice of colors for mushroom cloud—we want red; a soccer ball; a set of Magick cards; Trek uniform, size 3; *The Cat Wore Black Pajamas*."

"Oh, yeah, my cousin read that," Phillip said. "It's about a cat detective in Vietnam. It's the new one in that series of The Cat Wore mystery books. You know, *The Cat Wore Spats*, *The Cat in the Hawaiian Shirt*, *The Cat in the Cravat*. Those books."

Curtis continued the list, naming many other books in the mystery and science fiction genres. Also included were a Starbucks gift pack; an espresso coffee-making machine; an Investigative Reporter kit complete with tape recorder, binoculars, and a complete set of lock picks; six boxes of ebony dark chocolate Frango mints; bubble bath; stationery with kitties; and finally, "a Miss Cocoa to keep Mr. Coffee and Mrs. Tea company in the well-appointed gourmet kitchen, I suppose," Curtis concluded.

"That is a great many gifts!" Scrooge said. "Does everyone give so freely these days?"

"Oh, this is just the last-minute gifts," Curtis said. "They'd already done most of their shopping on-line or on the interactive cable, through catalogs, or the TV shopping channel. These are just the items they couldn't get that way."

"But, merciful heavens!" Scrooge said. "While I don't know what things cost these days, I would imagine the price of these items alone could have supported the Cratchetts for several years or paid the mortgage on one of my debtor's homes."

Curtis had to shout to be heard above the disembodied Christmas carols, the wails of tired children, the whirring of cash registers, and the rumble of voices from which an occasional "Excuse me," "Do you have this in a nine?" "May I please get by?" "Ooops," and "Watch where you're going" surfaced like passengers from a sinking ship just before they drowned in the tide.

"But where will we find all these things?" Scrooge asked.

Scrooge observed that Miriam tried to shrug, but while her shoulders did go up, she didn't have room to put them down again in the crush of people surrounding her.

The aisles were packed with goods and so were very narrow, and the people spilled off to either side. Slowly, and more or less together, Scrooge and his companions made their way through the emporium into a broad, enclosed pedestrian thoroughfare similar to the one he had seen in July, but with many more side streets and a much longer central avenue. Here the flow of people from the various doorways merely contributed to a great river of humanity surging along. The people were often attired in red and green, the cheery colors of Christmas, but they appeared harried, anxious, and distinctly *un*cheery, one and all. So heavily did the mob push that Scrooge found, to his unexpected satisfaction, that his own less-than-corporeal form was squeezed upward so that he was forced to float above the populace.

The air was thinner above the crowd, but since Scrooge no longer breathed, he scarcely minded. It was much better than having people walk through one. The others in his party appeared to be every bit as solid as the rest of the shoppers, but he supposed that if one was a ghost in actuality, one would remain a ghost in what the youngsters called virtual reality as well. His only change seemed to be that as a virtual ghost, he was more subject to being squeezed upward than to being walked through, or to walking through others. Really, this worked to his advantage.

From this lofty position, he could keep the others in sight as they dodged from one side of the avenue to the other, entering stores. He had little difficulty sailing under the wide high doorways well above the heads of the customers.

The young people, being geniuses, quickly found a way to use Scrooge's position to further their own ends.

"Eb, can you see the Barbie, God-Empress-of-the-Universe doll anywhere?" Miriam asked. He wasn't surprised she asked. She was not a tall woman, and many people towered over her, blocking her view of the goods.

"The doll section seems to be over to your right, my dear," he said, "and upon a very high shelf I see one last doll with an improbable approximation of a lady's—er—physique. She is wearing a most elaborate costume and beside her is a rocket. Perhaps Harald should go with you, as he is somewhat taller than you, and could fetch it down more easily?"

"Roger, Mr. S.," Harald said and the two of them, with a little further coaching, soon located the doll, took her to the counter, and found, to their relief, they also had a virtual credit card with which to pay for her.

Similarly, Scrooge was able to help them secure other purchases. From the toy store, they fought their way to the music store; from the music store to the bookstore; from the bookstore to the household goods store; winning every step, swimming with the tide at times so swiftly as to be swept past their goal, at other times swimming against it so that it seemed each inch had to be gained many times over before progress was made. Not only that, but sometimes several stores had to be checked before the desired object could be obtained. If it were not found in this mall, Scrooge had no doubt that the penalty would be that they must forever roam the malls of America until they acquired that final gift. It reminded him uncomfortably of Marley's chains and cash boxes.

The young people looked very weary, and with every new purchase, the bundle of things grew that they had to haul down the long aisles, safeguarding it from the depredations of the mob.

At last, triumphantly, Harald placed the last gift, the Miss Cocoa, on the counter at the store. Then there remained only the task of carrying it all back the way they had come, relocating their vehicle, and braving the highways once more.

They were young, and not so daunted as he would have been, but they all looked ready for the knacker to take them to the glue yard by the time they regained the sidewalk outside of the store through which they had originally entered.

"Well done, my friends, well done," Scrooge said, applauding.

"Good thing someone still has the oomph left to clap," Sheryl said. "You see why people don't look forward to Christmas so much now, Eb?"

"Surely a Christmas so hard-won must be all the sweeter?" Scrooge asked with more optimism than he actually felt was called for.

"Easy for you to say, since you could fly," Sheryl said. "Don't suppose it occured to you to let us fly, too."

"We couldn't have tried taking off and landing in that crowd without standing on someone else's head," Phillip pointed out.

"Well, to paraphrase Tiny Tim, God bless you, every one," Scrooge said, trying to buck them up.

"Yeah, well, tiptoe through the tulips to you, too, bud," Sheryl said.

They managed to get through the rest of the program with only a little more difficulty. Two purse snatchings and an attempted carjacking in the parking lot were foiled by security officers, which added interest to the journey. As soon as they found their vehicle again and Curtis started it, they were whisked back to the little office and the young people were neatly ejected from the program. They seemed none the worse for wear and quite relieved and happy to be back, bearing none of the merchandise they had gathered with such difficulty.

Scrooge cleared his throat. "An intriguing diversion, my friends, but the point is not for you to show me why you have just cause to dislike Christmas, as you seem to believe, but for me to convince your employer that she should regard it with more favor. Therefore, I believe it's time to move on to a different guise, if I'm to use my own experience as a model. Something stern and implacable. My own Christmas Future was, of course, death himself."

"Trite," John said, yawning to stress his point. "Stereotypical. Conventional."

"But scary," Curtis said. "You gotta admit it's scary."

"What's like death only more with it, more now, more happening, you know?" Melody asked.

Sheryl shrugged. "All that occurs to me is taxes. And Monica's been there and done that."

"Yeah," Harald said. "She's done unto others already okay, but has she had it done unto her?"

"I like it. I like it a lot," Curtis said.

Phillip was grinning from ear to ear. Which was unfortunate since he had just picked up a piece of cold pizza and was chewing it, even as he grinned.

"Scrooge, baby, I believe the most effective thing would be if you examined the wonderful world of cross-dressing, don't you think, folks?" Sheryl asked. The others nodded.

Once the morph was complete, they spent several hilarious moments giving Scrooge pointers on how to act more like their employer, but Scrooge discouraged this. It reminded him uncomfortably of how his nephew had mocked him at that long-ago Christmas party. Instead, he enlisted the assistance of one of them in a new scheme to jar the heiress to Databanks from her complacency.

Fourteen

~

Monica Banks stood regarding Monica Banks with an expression of distaste and barely concealed hostility. "For heaven's sake, Miss Banks, please get up and face this in a professional manner. Your account has come due. It is time to face the consequences. No need to make this any more difficult than it need be by delaying the process further."

Scrooge had spoken these same words, inserting different names, many times before, and found that he had no problem imitating the professional demeanor of Monica Banks, IRS agent, so creditably that even Monica Banks, computer firm CEO, could not tell the difference. She looked extremely confused and disoriented.

Once David had helped morph Scrooge so that he physically and vocally resembled Monica Banks as she had been in her former role, he had slipped into Monica's apartment and pressed the "Enter" button on her computer, and by holding onto the couch when he pressed, had entered both himself and Monica, as well as the apartment, into the program. Then he had morphed himself into an ageless, faceless, conservatively dressed federal enforcement agent so he could, incognito, accompany Monica and Scrooge.

"Excuse me," the Monica on the couch said. "Do you have an appointment? I was expecting someone else. I was told that the Spirit of Christmas Future was going to be paying me a visit."

"Precisely," Monica in the business suit, with the clipboard, accompanied by the looming agent with handcuffs, said impatiently. "Come along, now. It won't look good on your record if you stall."

"I'm not stalling," Monica said, getting to her feet and this time, forewarned by previous experiences, prudently slipping into sheepskin-lined moccasins and a heavy sweater. "It's just—well, you're me."

"Don't think that gives you any special privileges," the spirit said sternly. "There's an account to be settled, and I'm the best one for the job precisely because I never take prisoners, so to speak. Come on."

Despite the spirit's claim that she never took prisoners, she motioned the enforcement officer, who clasped the handcuffs, locking one cuff on each Monica, so the pair appeared to be Siamese twins joined at the wrist. Then the spirit whisked the Databanks heiress through the door without bothering to open it, took to the air like Wonder Woman in a far less alluring than usual power suit and sensible shoes, while Monica trailed in her wake. Once beyond the Databanks campus, the spirit circled like a vulture over the city, apparently deliberating where would be the best place to begin horrifying her double into having a merry Christmas.

Monica really had only the spirit's word for it that they were in Christmas future. Seattle looked much the same as it had in her earlier encounter. The same star at the top of the Bon Marche, the same flags, the same red and green lights on the Space Needle, the same white lights in the trees, the same horse carriages at Westlake, the same garlands at Pioneer Square, the same Christmas ships out in Elliot Bay.

"Spirit," she said, "This uh—audit you're conducting. It's only of estimated returns for the future, isn't it? Things are changeable. I have already formed some plans as regards the little Timmons girl that may significantly alter my debit and credit columns in the future."

"Miss Banks, what you wish to do or do not wish to do in the future is none of my concern. My concern is only with demonstrating to you the consequences of your actions to date, extrapolated to their most logical nth degree and decimal points to the millionth place. I must tell you that in all surveys conducted, the chances of a woman of your advanced years significantly altering her personality and behavior are almost nil." Where Scrooge got this information, he had no idea, but it seemed like the right thing to say. Perhaps the Program Manager also provided his supernaturally enhanced morph with a bit of jargon to add versimilitude to his present personna.

"Can't teach an old dog new tricks, huh?" Monica asked. "If you believe that, why not let me stumble on my merry way instead of showing me all of these people and events? I know you, Monica. If you didn't think it would make a difference, you wouldn't waste your time."

Monica-the-spirit looked down her glasses at Monica-the-mortal. "That remains to be seen," the spirit said. "Now then, what do you suggest we see first?"

"I want to see the Timmons girl."

"I'm afraid that won't be possible," the spirit said in Monica's own best, clipped, official voice.

"What do you mean that won't be possible? I *can* do something for this child. This is a bright and perceptive child, an intelligent child, and she deserves the chance I can give her. I demand to speak to your superior. I demand . . ."

Then they were once more inside the Timmons apartment. The table was set, and an origami tree, smashed and messy and stained around the edges, made a centerpiece. The only straight chair in the room was vacant.

The broken television had been replaced and occupied the space opposite the table. Noah and Jamie stared into it, watching *National Lampoon's Christmas* while Brianna plopped the tuna and noodle casserole on the table. "Daddy, Jamie, come to the table. Tiffany and her husband are going to be here soon."

Monica turned to the spirit. "Is that all? Tina's mother got married. That's why she's not there. Right? You had me going there—"

"What do you care?" her own mouth asked her coldly. "The brat helped trick you. She violated rules. See the unemployment papers laying on the television? They have Noah Timmons's name on them. He's out of a job."

"I wasn't going to fire him!" Monica protested, but the door to the apartment swung open then and Tiffany entered, trailed by a man sporting very shiny white shoes and matching belt, several gold chains that glinted among his thick, dark chest hairs, a silk shirt in a western pattern. He had a bored look on his face. Tiffany was pregnant, and her face and ankles were bloated, though her wrists looked bony and her skin sallow and lifeless. Faint yellow marks on her arms, old bruises, gave her an unhealthy, mottled look.

Her father tore himself away from the television and rose to hug her. "Baby, there you are. We were afraid you wouldn't make it."

"We can't stay, Daddy. Louie and I got a dinner date with his business associates. Anyway, you know how I get here. I can't hardly stand to see her little chair . . ." and she began crying.

"Dammit, Tiffany, I told you if we came over here you'd start in again," her husband said, hauling her roughly out of the room. "We'll see ya, Pop. Merry Christmas."

"Get me out of here this instant," Monica told the spirit. "I can't stand to see the chair, either. Or that horrible man. Or this hideous apartment. It seemed so homey before, but now it's just—" She shivered. "Sordid. Tawdry. Depressing. What's wrong with Jamie? Even for a kid watching TV he looks—well, maybe he's stoned. I guess so. Why doesn't Noah notice? What's Brianna so mad about? And why don't any of them seem to notice that Tiffany's husband obviously is mistreating her? I thought this was the family values portion of your program. What's wrong with these people? Do they think Tina would like them this way?"

"You're in such a fine position to judge others, aren't you?" the ghost said nastily. "At least they're not out making other people miserable for the holidays."

"What I do or don't do has no bearing on their situation," Monica said, though she suspected the point was arguable. "I told you I'll change, but you don't believe me, in spite of what I've been through with the three of you spirits. Give me a break. Show me something a little more upbeat."

The miserable apartment melted away to be replaced by a large room with a sweeping view of the bay and people in beautiful, casually dressy attire chatting, eating, and drinking, admiring the objets d'art and listening to a string quartet playing discreet Christmas carols.

"Is this more like it?" the spirit asked.

Monica nodded warily. She realized the wariness was appropriate when she heard Senator Johansen's voice rise above the crowd. "Ladies and gentlemen, I'd like to propose a toast to our mutual benefactress, Monica Banks."

There were low murmurs and the clinking of glasses. Near the ghost, a red-haired man who looked familiar said, "I wonder what Money Banks would say if she knew the senator publicly considered her a benefactress after he helped break Databanks."

"I don't know, but I can't say that in the end she did me any harm," said the woman, someone who looked a bit like Sheryl, only older, richer, and more sophisticated. "If she hadn't fired me, I'd never have gone on to form my own company."

Then there was no mistaking it. The second man in the group was definitely that Dave guy from marketing. He certainly looked propserous and pleased with himself. "Yeah, well, I'd have never joined up with Harald and Miriam in merchandizing their little invention nobody thought would amount to anything. Did I tell you that Melody and I have to buy a second house in California now just so we can keep up with the telemarketing end of things?"

"Yeah, but it was me she did the biggest favor," Sheryl said. "If she hadn't booted my butt out, I'd have still been there holding onto my stocks when the feds came and took it all away."

Monica looked back at the spirit. "T-took it all away? How? Why?"

"I don't have that information immediately accessible, but wasn't Senator Johansen your attorney before he went into politics, and didn't his firm continue to deal with your tax problems, etcetera?"

"Oh brother!" Monica said. "Don't tell me I forget all of what happens here tonight to the extent that I don't fire that snake . . . Or is it too late?"

The spirit who looked so much like her shrugged her own shrug. It was contemptuous.

"Well, at least I made these people happy."

"By failing to recognize their ability, alienating them, and driving them off into other enterprises, which, given their talents and intelligence, paid them more handsomely than you were doing. That's quite an accomplishment," the spirit said acerbically.

"I think we'd better leave now."

"Just a moment."

"Where's Wayne?" asked Curtis Lu, who joined the group of his former colleagues.

"Oh, you know. I invited him," said another man—John, John Beardesley, that was it. He was a debugger or something. "But he's heavy into telecommuting for everything since his mom died. I don't think he'd stay long at any party that had Johansen at it, either. Wayne's not even a *fiscal* Republican. You know that."

"Mrs. Reilly died? Oh dear. Spirit, we have to go see Wayne. He adored his mother—not that he was a mama's boy, or anything like that, but she was a nice lady. Please, let's get out of here and go see him."

"Very well," the spirit said. "It's on our way."

Monica wondered what her guide meant by that.

This night was wet and cold, and yet there was no fire in Wayne's fireplace, though he sat at his computer in the den as he had before. Instead of books and papers littering the floor, an avalanche of wadded Kleenex overflowed the wastebasket and desk to all but bury a red-nosed, bleary-eyed Wayne. He was much grayer than when she had seen him last and his beard, which was several days old, had far too much white in it. He still wore pajamas and a robe, and Monica wondered when the last time was that he'd worn anything else.

He sneezed, blew his nose, and typed a few words into

the computer. Then he sneezed and blew his nose again, and wiped his eyes with the back of his hand.

"Poor guy," Monica said. "Guess this Christmas isn't going to be any fun at all for him."

"What's the difference?" the spirit said harshly, sounding so much like Monica herself that the heiress cringed. "He's always been a bit of a sob sister anyway. Now he's got something to cry about."

"Didn't you hear what they said at the party? He's just lost his mother. And he's all alone."

"He doesn't have to be. Surely with his millions he could buy love."

Monica lingered near him and put her hand on his shoulder, but she knew he couldn't feel it. The spirit stood nearby, tapping her toe.

Finally, Monica turned and asked with a sigh, "Are we going to go back to visit the people Wayne corresponds with? Is that why we're here?"

The spirit shook her head. "That is all in what is now the past. There is something else here you ought to see."

"How much time has passed? When will this happen?"

The spirit sniffed. "I'm not at liberty to divulge that information. We like to keep the element of surprise on our side in order to ensure that the subject keeps his or her affairs and files current and up to date at all times. Mr. Reilly is setting a good example. He is now making an entry in his electronic journal. You will notice that he uses an off-line machine and stores all information on a removable disk for security reasons. He did this after having pieces of his diary copied and presented as evidence in the legal actions against Databanks and Monica Banks, CEO, Databanks."

It was Monica's turn to sniff. "I wouldn't think you'd approve of that. Privacy, I mean."

"You're the one who sounds disapproving, which is odd, since your company was the one that created the software to invade Mr. Reilly's machine."

"I don't want to invade Wayne's privacy," she said, feeling the heat rise in her face as she thought of one particular message he'd been sending on her previous visit. "It might be . . . private."

The spirit ignored her and drew her into Wayne's machine.

Monica immediately looked for the dates on the entries and the spirit, with a smirk, stabbed her finger in the air and produced little bars of color over that portion of the screen above each entry.

Monica glared at her and the spirit's smirk deepened. Monica made a silent vow never to smirk at anyone ever again unless she deeply, passionately loathed and despised that person.

The first entry appeared as a mural, spreading out before her.

"Missed Christmas with Ma. The airport was socked in, and there was no way to get out. Monica turned me down again, too. Oh well, there's always another Christmas, I guess."

The next entry was a forwarded file from an on-line tabloid. "Government Forecloses on Databanks—Money Left With Only One Mansion to Her Name."

"That's not fair," Monica said. "I only have one mansion and that's the one Doug built by the lake. It's much too big for me, and the whole thing is computer operated. I can hardly open a cabinet because I haven't figured out the controls. Up until I inherited it, I couldn't even afford a home of my own. These people forget that I *worked* for my money."

"Too bad for you, but I don't think they forgot a thing," the spirit said nastily, and pointed to an issue of *People* magazine with a picture of Monica on the cover. "Monica—Money—Banks, What Next for the Diabolic Dimpled Dumpling of Databanks?" The index promised articles titled, " 'I Remember Monica—the Year the IRS Took My Farm' and Other Atrocity Stories by Those the Former Tax Termagent Ruined." The spirit clicked to a picture of seventy-four-year-old former farmer Homer Pewterbottom, who was quoted as saying, "When I saw that that nasty tax woman what took my farm had inherited millions, I said to Obesella, that's my pig, 'Obesella,' I said, 'That there is just another case of good things happenin' to bad people.' But I reckon she's got her comeuppance now and I say good riddance to bad rubbish."

"I'm surprised the government doesn't step in and sue for libel," Monica said hotly. "I was only doing my job. These people weren't paying taxes they legally owed."

"Did you try to work with them? Did you cooperate with them in any way possible to ascertain your figures were correct? Did you even listen to them?"

"No, but that wasn't my . . . I suppose I might have been a little harder than I should have been with some people who were honest and deserved more consideration. But you meet so many deadbeats, you get tired of worrying about who's trying to trick you. There are guidelines, you know."

"Yes, and they are interpreted differently from agent to agent. You had another nickname in your office, didn't you, Monica? Because you were the most rigid and punitive of all the people there. What was it, Monica? It wasn't Money, was it?"

"No, it—"

"Rhymed with Banks, didn't it?"

"Yes—"

"Something large and hard and unrelenting . . ."

"Tank," Monica said. "They called me Tank Banks. Thank God the press never got hold of that."

"Oh, but they did. See here on page forty-seven?"

Monica groaned.

"Ah—look at this. '60 *Minutes* on Get a Life' it says here by this little picture of—what would you say that is, Ms. Banks?"

"It's a film clip," Monica said tiredly.

"Let's see."

"This is Donald Sortoff for 60 *Minutes*," the earnest man on the clip said. "Earlier this year, Databanks Corporation not only released a new type of network communications management, but made sure each and every computer in their affiliated hardware companies came off the assembly line equipped with this tool. The product claimed to be a revolutionary way to tend to every phase of your business and personal life via telecommunication. Soon, people who used this began to notice that their affairs were not only public, they were being monitored in a 1984-esque fashion by government computers trained to pick up certain words and phrases and act, in effect, as a sort of KGB here in the U.S. We go now to talk to—"

The film went fuzzy for a moment and then Sortoff and his microphone appeared outside Doug's mansion. "Databanks, as we learned earlier this week, has claimed bankruptcy after most of its assets had been seized by the IRS, an ironic twist of fate, since the controversial CEO of the company, Monica 'Money' Banks, was herself once an IRS auditor. This home, estimated to be worth upwards of twelve million dollars, is still in the possession of Monica Banks as it is her domicile and cannot, under law, be seized. We knocked on her door earlier, but no one answered. It is believed that Banks is inside, secluded from the press, but we were unable to find anyone to talk to. There are no servants. The eccentric Banks heiress prefers it that way. Former employees say she has an exaggerated sense of privacy, almost a paranoia—"

Monica shivered. "How can they say that when they really are all against me? Spirit, none of this has to happen, does it? I don't have to produce Get a Life—"

"You have a contract. You have obligations. You have a deadline."

"You have a discouraging way of putting things."

"Yes, I do, don't you?" the spirit said with another nasty smirk. "Shall we see what Wayne's up to now?"

They emerged from within the computer again to find

Wayne writing another message on his on-line computer. "I know she doesn't want to see me anymore or anybody else, but I've asked her to Christmas dinner every year since we were kids and I'm not going to stop now. Flu or no flu, I'll ask her. All she can do is say no like she always does, and I'm used to that."

"Way to go, Paddy," the person on the other end replied. "Go for it. Merry Christmas."

"Merry Christmas," Wayne typed and flipped back out to compose another letter. "Dear Moni," it began, but Monica read no more as she and the spirit were swooshed once more through the lines connecting the machines and she found herself and her other self arriving in a cold, dark room from the dark, cold monitor of a seemingly dead computer.

Fortunately for them both, the spectral Monica shone with her own eldritch light by which they could see their surroundings. "You know this place?" the spirit asked.

"Of course I do. This is Doug's house. Well, my house really. I've been intending to block this room off."

"But the computer is here," the ghost said.

"There's a computer in every room of this house, sometimes more than one. I feel like I have no privacy. That's why I fired the servants. I can wash my own underwear, thank you, though I admit I've had trouble locating the washer and dryer. To tell you the truth, I haven't spent much time here. I find it . . . large. It was Doug's dream house, not mine."

"Hmph," said the ghost. "Why are there no windows?"

"A lot of it is underground. Doug said it saves energy."

She crossed her arms and hugged herself. Though she couldn't actually feel the cold with her skin, she felt it just the same. "I just think it's dark and gloomy unless you put in a lot of that full spectrum light, which is expensive."

"He was a multimillionaire."

"No excuse to be a spendthrift," Monica said. As the spirit drifted to one of the frost-rimed walls and pointed out the icicles that had formed from condensation on the chandelier, Monica added, "Of course, one can always take thrift too far. Looks like I overdid it here."

The spirit nodded, but just then there came a heavy thumping and bumping and the beams from two flashlights flooded the room as the door caved in under attack from without. The spirit increased her candlepower so that beyond the flashlight beams, Monica saw two rough-looking people in stocking caps and tattered jackets burst into the room. One methodically began filling garbage sacks with the room's portable contents while the other one unplugged the computer and its parts and loaded them onto a shopping cart.

"Thieves," Monica said. "Help! Police! Call 911."

"With what?" the ghost asked. "There's no power here— or why would the room be so cold and dark? And even if there were, no one would hear you."

When the thieves finished looting the place, laughing and making fun of the things they stuck into their bags, they began smashing things, and a third person, someone Monica had seen under different circumstances only recently, appeared with a spray can. "Hey, Money Banks!" He hollered, pounding on the wall, a pounding that was enthusiastically joined by the others, who shouted threats and ugly names through the door with crude, frightening laughter until the first figure waved them quiet. "We could use jobs! How about you hire us as your new decorators, huh?" he asked, and as they all laughed and capered to the partnership of their own hugely exaggerated shadows, he scrawled an obscenity across the wall with great loops of paint.

"Let's get out of here," Monica said.

"We can't go the way we came," the spirit pointed out. "We'll have to go out through the house, or until we find a computer still intact, if we're to take the ethernet."

But the rooms they went through were worse: the kitchen sink frozen and fouled, filthy water all over the floor, and at some point, a fire had flared to burn itself out on the fireproof exteriors. The bathrooms were unspeakable, and over every surface were the angry graffiti. In the next two rooms, an assortment of people camped out in the damage and she saw her clothes, bedclothes, and draperies used as bedding and her furniture as firewood for fires built on the floors.

At last they stood outside in the cold wind and rain, watching it pour through the broken glass in the front of the house. The lake tossed fitfully, dark with whitecaps, and seemed to be groping with lopping waves for the broken entrance.

"Spirit, one of those people—I thought I recognized him."

"Now, where would you meet that sort of person?"

"It looked like Jamie, Tina Timmons's uncle. Where am I in all of this, spirit, that these people treat my house this way? Am I in jail? Nothing in Wayne's diary indicated it."

Two dark-clad figures emerged from the broken glass and the one who looked like Jamie said, "Whew, man, can you believe the smell in there?"

His companion laughed. "Yeah, man, her ritzy joint isn't so ritzy anymore, is it?"

"No, man, but it's coming from the part of the house we couldn't break into. It smells *bad,* man."

"Maybe she ain't felt like takin' no bath since the water pipes busted," the other one suggested in a mincing voice.

"I dunno. I say let's get out of here." Jamie's two companions loaded their loot into the car, but Jamie said, "I gotta go meet somebody. We can divvy it up later."

"Fer sure, man. We'll save you some. Definitely," they said, and spun away in a fury of squealing rubber.

Monica looked at the ghost in horror. "Am I still in that house? With it being destroyed all around me? With all those people camping out, pounding on the walls, pipes bursting?"

"Let's follow young Jamie and see where he goes, shall we?" the ghost suggested.

The boy walked for blocks and blocks until he came to the University District, where he went to a pay phone and stuck what looked like a credit card in a slot. "Hello, is this KSBS-TV? I wanna talk to Bambi Billings herself. I got a little scoop here. She is? Hi, Bambi, I always watch you on TV." The kid sounded like he was about to ask for her autograph, but then apparently Bambi Billings told him what a busy woman she was because he turned surly again. "Yeah, well for your information, lady, I do have information for you. There's a big story at the Banks mansion. Somebody broke in there, and it smells like somebody died. Anybody seen old Money Banks lately? Maybe you people better check. Sounds like a story to me. No, I ain't gonna introduce myself while you get the police to come and find my butt, but it was nice speaking with you, too. Bye."

"Oh, spirit," Monica said. "I don't want to stay here waiting for the vultures to come. Let's leave. Let's go back to Wayne's. He looks so sick and . . . old . . . and—"

"You don't have to give me excuses, Miss Banks. Don't forget to whom you are speaking. I quite see through your lies." And she and the spirit, to whom she was still handcuffed, were swirled aloft with the boiling clouds, the roaring winds, and the driving rain. The enforcement agent followed at a discreet distance.

They sank down through the roof of Wayne's house and into his den. The telephone was ringing. "Hello. Yes, it's me. I have a cold so I just *sound* like Johnny Cash. Who's this? Oh, yeah, sure I remember you. Carl from testing who went over to do the news for KSBS. *What* break-in at the Banks mansion? *What*—did she call the police? Was she even home? Then who called you? But the police confirmed this anonymous tip, did they? No, I haven't heard from her since she went to ground. I did just try to raise her by E-mail, but she hasn't answered, though I can't exactly say that amazes me. Look, how about I meet you over there? Okay, I'm on my way."

He left the den for the hallway, pulled on a raincoat over his pajamas and robe, and stuffed his sockless feet into short rubber boots. He did pause to cram a wad of Kleenex in his raincoat pocket before he slid into the seat of his teal green Saturn. He didn't see the Monicas cuffed together in the backseat nor the enforcement agent, who no longer resembled Dave from marketing, in the front.

It was early and the streets were almost deserted, so he came to no harm despite driving like a jet pilot from his house to the long drive leading to the smoke-fogged entrance of the Banks mansion. He had to park behind a long line of police cars, ambulances, a fire truck, and the KSBS news van. The driveway was full of water and the once well-kept grounds were clogged with half-drowned, tall weeds and overgrown flowers and shrubs. Floodlights illuminated the gaping hole in the front of the house. Firemen were winding their hose back on their truck while police bundled the squatters Monica and the spirit had observed earlier into squad cars. Other police and firemen were picking their way carefully through the building.

Meanwhile, an anchorwoman in a smart trench coat and wearing a patently false expression of concern and dismay, stuck a microphone in Wayne's face. "Mr. Reilly, I'm Bambi Billings from KSBS-TV news. Would you give our viewers your impression of the terrible disaster that seems to have overtaken the Banks empire? Were you not once a partner in this empire until you were cheated out of your share by the late Douglas Banks, and were you not one of the few people who had a personal friendship with a woman who's become known as the Queen of Mean of the computer world, Monica 'Money' Banks, herself?"

Wayne looked as if he were about to bolt. Then he said brusquely but with a little smile, "It's a real mess, yes, no, and maybe. Excuse me." With that he pushed past her and made his way to the front of the building. A policeman started to stop him, but after a few words, he called another officer over to guard the entrance and preceded Wayne into the building himself.

"Do I have to go back in there?" Monica asked the ghost.

The ghost didn't speak this time but pulled her back inside the building, through the rubble, now soaked from the fire hose, to a door to which the firefighters were applying the Jaws of Life device. The door gave, but behind it was a barricade of furniture, which they had to push past as well. Those who weren't wearing masks were holding pieces of cloth to their faces, and Wayne pulled out his handful of Kleenex to do likewise, turning his nose away.

"Mr. Reilly, I hope you're ready for this, sir," one of the men said. "I've smelled this kind of thing before, and I can tell you it won't be pretty."

It wasn't. The men almost stumbled over the corpse, which was rolled in a sleeping bag on the couch that had been added to the barricade. The room was otherwise bare, except for the fireplace, which held pieces of wood from broken furniture.

"I'm not going to look," Monica said. "It's just some vagrant who broke into my house, isn't it? Tell me it is, spirit."

The ghost nodded toward Wayne, who took a brief look over the back of the couch and recoiled, burying his face in the Kleenex.

"Sir, we realize this is unpleasant, but we need to know. Is the deceased here Monica Banks?"

Wayne nodded, then ducked into a corner of the room and threw up.

"God, I must be a real mess," Monica said, shuddering. "Get me out of here, spirit. You've showed me my death. I'm impressed. I want to wake up now."

"What? Without realizing your full impact on your fellow beings? Oh, no, I can't permit you to be so modest. Come. KSBS is getting their story, and we can watch the news on Wayne's television."

By the time they returned to Wayne's house, without him this time, since he had lingered for whatever reason Monica couldn't bear to imagine, KSBS was indeed airing their morning program. "Good morning and happy holidays from KSBS-TV," the handsome, serious news anchor said. He had a cheerful Christmas tie with patterns of presents on it to set off his tasteful, dark blue suit. "I'm Treat Ramsey, bringing you this special report on the death of Databanks heiress Monica Banks, also known by the nickname Money Banks. The badly decomposed body of Ms. Banks was discovered a short time ago by firefighters and police in the ruins of the palatial Lake Washington home she inherited from her late brother Doug, founder of the Databanks empire. Her identity was confirmed by Doug's former partner and the former neighbor of both Doug and Monica Banks, Wild Web founder Wayne Reilly. We now take you to Bambi Billings on location at the devastated Banks mansion. Hi, Bambi. It looks wet out there."

"It certainly is, Treat," said Bambi, from her little video box superimposed on the KSBS newsroom. The wind tore through her hair dramatically. "But rescuers have been tireless emptying the Banks compound of the many people who have camped out in the safety of its walls."

"Before we go into that, Bambi, can you tell us something about the cause of Monica Banks's death? Is foul play suspected? Was the body in any way molested?"

"Oh, turn this off!" Monica said. "This is too tacky! He's practically slobbering right there in front of the television audience!"

"He is not," the spirit said firmly.

"Well, then he's inciting the public to slobber."

"No, Treat, according to rescuers, Banks seems to have died of exposure, despite being inside her own home. What they believe happened is that with her assets frozen by the courts from her recent legal battles with the government, the woman known as Money no longer had enough money to maintain the huge mansion she inherited from her brother's estate. If she vacated for any reason, the government had a right to seize the building, so she stayed on long after the telephone, power, and gas were shut off. From the flooding in the building, it appears that the water was not shut off until later. Meanwhile, Banks, friendless and with no one to turn to, stayed in one room of the vast mansion, feeding furniture to the fireplace and living on canned goods. At some point, the dark, empty, seemingly deserted building, now devoid of the protection of its electronic security system, invited squatters, thieves, and vandals. Sergeant John Tremont of the King County Police, can you tell us anything about the occupation of the Banks mansion?"

A trim man in his late forties, wearing a slicker and a plastic cover over his hat, spoke gravely into the microphone. "Well, Bambi, it's an ongoing investigation at present, but it seems pretty clear at this point that the occupation has gone on for some weeks. Vandals beat in first the outer windows of the house, then the various doors as they penetrated the interior of the home. Some seem to have been only in search of shelter, but others were there to loot. Still, there was so much to steal and the doors were so strong that it seems to have taken them some time to make their way to the interior of the house, where Banks had barricaded herself. No doubt she started out living in more than one room, but as she heard the noises and couldn't make it to the outer entrance without going past the intruders—"

"What noises would those have been, Sergeant?"

"Objects breaking, the booming of doors giving way, that sort of thing. Also some of the squatters report loud parties, obscene language, and threats made by other intruders against Miss Banks, some of them pretty graphic. I guess the lady was so scared to come out that she was pretty much scared to death."

"Scared to death," Bambi repeated, dwelling with relish on each sensational word. "At one time the richest woman in this city, possibly in the country, ladies and gentlemen, has just died alone, cold, and probably hungry, listening to the threats of people who seemed to hate her. She died, you heard it, scared to death. What does that say about our society, eh, Treat?"

"Let's see if you made it to the radio as well, shall we?" asked the ghost, shutting the television off with a flick of her finger. With another flick, the stereo system lit up and a popular talk radio announcer's voice came on.

"Hey, did you hear that Money Banks was found all dead and icky in her big old house last night? Which brings us to an interesting question. Even if Banks is cremated, what're they going to do with the ashes? I mean, who'd want 'em? Give us your answers—*now*.

"Hel-lo, this is Jack the Jackal, KLYMX—that's Kli-max—FM. Merry Christmas. What's on your mind?"

"That rich woman who died was a tax collector. They could let her fertilize a potted plant at the federal building."

"Recycle her, huh? Good idea. Next. Merry Christmas, Jack the Jackal here."

"You know, that woman had every advantage, and all she ever did was make other people miserable. I think she should just be flushed down the toilet, since she treated everyone else like that's where they belonged."

"Peace on earth to you, too, ma'am. Next. This is Jack the Jackal. Merry Christmas. What's on your mind?"

"About the Banks broad: You know when they burn old money at the banks? They should just burn old Money Banks along with it and do with her whatever they do with the dead bills. She'd like that."

"Well, Merry Christmas to you, too, you sick sucker . . ."

If Monica had been in tears before, she was hysterical now, crying so hard she didn't hear the next answer. "Spirit, take me home, please. Don't let this be how it is. I'm not like this. These people don't even know me and listen to how much they hate me."

"They might hate you worse if they did know you."

"Whose side are you on, anyway?" she cried, and threw herself as far to the spirit's feet as she could go, still hand-cuffed to her. "Oh, please let me wake up and have a chance to change some things. There's so much I didn't realize. So much I didn't know."

"Ignorance is no excuse," the spirit said. "That's what you used to tell anyone who asked you for mercy."

"But I've learned so much," Monica pleaded. "I can fix it. I really can. I can learn. Please, spirit, I have changed, I have. . . ."

Fifteen

~~~~~

Monica awoke to find herself clutching the French Provincial dust ruffle on the sofa, the words, "I have . . ." on her lips. She looked around her at the bleak, sleek little office apartment, at the screen saver building castles out of Legos on her computer screen, at the television, where Bambi Billings's cheerful face was mouthing muted words. She immediately clicked off the television and picked up the phone, dialing the time and weather number. "Merry Christmas," it said. "The time is seven o'clock A.M. The temperature is thirty-two degrees."

"I have a lot to do!" Monica exclaimed to herself. She dialed the extension of the project coordinator for the Get a Life project. "I want the whole team assembled in my office in fifteen minutes," she told the fellow without waiting for a reply.

"Now for good old Bob," she said, dialing the senator's home number.

"Hello?"

"This is Monica Banks calling for Bob," she said. "May I speak to him?"

"This is the maid, madam. Senator and Mrs. Banks are on their way to Hong Kong on business. Would you care to leave a message?"

"No, no, I'll take care of it later," she said, disappointed. Ebenezer Scrooge had been able to get more immediate results. "Now then, a little last-minute Christmas shopping."

She was still on the phone when she heard the scuffle of feet in the outer office. "I'll get back to you," she said to the phone, hung up, and marched to the door. She flung it open and glared at the employees gathered around.

"So," she said. "You thought you would have a little fun at old Money Banks's expense, did you? You and your supernatural friends." They gaped at her and started jabbering at once, but she held up her hand. "You've been sitting around here on *my* dime all through this holiday with the computers down, doing absolutely nothing. Well, it ends now."

Curtis Lu cleared his throat so hard his Adam's apple threatened to bounce out the crown of his head. "But, Ms. Banks, what about Get a Life?"

"Get a Life is a nonstarter as you very well know, Mr. Lu, as all of you know and—" she pointed her finger accusingly at him, "tried to tell me all along. I'm pulling the plug, refunding the monies. This means cutbacks, of course," and she gave them her nastiest smile.

The team groaned.

"Unless, of course, we can quickly come up with another big new consumer-based program that will have such appeal as to make up the losses. And whether or not we do, you people are just kidding yourselves if you think I'm going to take the losses and risks of this business all by myself. From now on, all Databanks personnel, starting with yourselves, will jointly share the majority of corporate stock holdings. That is, anyone will who wishes to exercise the stock options you will find in your virtual Christmas stockings, as soon as someone shows me how to create them. And of course, the papers will have to be drawn up. Can anybody recommend a good lawyer?"

The team began applauding, and Melody impulsively left her spot by the door and enveloped Monica in an enthusiastic hug, which was immediately joined by everyone else.

"We knew you'd come through it okay, Money Banks," Curtis said.

"You did? You weren't just laughing at me when you saw me in Christmas Present?"

"Nah," said Harald. "We thought you just hated us because we were geeks but we saw—at least I did—in Christmas Past that you were a geek, too. That was what made you so prickly. It was just that Doug outgeeked you, and it gave you—"

"A geek block," Miriam finished up.

"But we're not gonna let you get away with that, Monica," Sheryl said sternly. "If you're going to be one of the major shareholders here, you gotta know the territory."

"Which *we* happen to know rather well," Phillip said, hooking a modest thumb around his suspenders.

"So, I've been thinking, gang. Especially now that Monica here has made us all associates, how about we start an educational program ASAP to bring the boss up to speed on what she is now going to be doing for a living?"

"Good idea, Sheryl. We could call it Operation Ground Up because she'd be learning everything from zip. Are you willing, boss?"

Monica nodded, her eyes shining with tears. "If you think I can even ever begin to understand it. I've always known I wasn't a genius like—"

"Cut that out. Anybody who can understand the ins and outs of income tax is plenty bright enough to understand anything. You've clearly got the math gene."

"Listen, I was wondering. One other thing. I thought at first I wanted to sell Doug's mansion to put some of the money back into the company, but now it occurs to me— well, I don't want to say anything yet, but any of you who are good teachers may have an extra assignment. However, that is not why I've called you all together now." She assumed her General-Patton-at-ease stance. "Right now, I need your help making pickups and deliveries of Christmas gifts and dinners for some people. Some of the store managers are driving delivery trucks themselves, but we have to go pick up the rest of it. Are you with me?"

Curtis snapped a salute. "Yes, Fearless Leader."

"My Christmas is your Christmas to command, Fearless Leader," Dave mimicked.

"*Except* you, David. You are to go here and collect this." She gave him a sheet of paper. "And then go home and spend all of your remaining time plus two weeks comp time with your daughter."

When the troops dispersed a moment later, Monica was still blushing from the kiss Dave planted on her before he left.

Sixteen

⌁

Early Christmas morning, Tina was up and looked in her empty stocking. No candy. No kitty. She wasn't surprised. Her mama had heard her get up and scooped her into her arms and said, "Oh, honey, I'm sorry. Santa missed you this year, didn't he?"

Tina gave Mama a hug. "No, Mama, he didn't. I had so much fun playing with Doug and making that present for Miss Banks it was a really, really good Christmas. Almost like I'd been making my own present."

"You tell 'em, tiger," said Uncle Jamie, making mock punching motions at her, which she parried. "I really like my origami Mechanoman, Tina, especially the way you made it out of the Sunday funnies."

Grandpa appeared at the door of the room he and Jamie shared. He was still in his undershirt and pajama bottoms, stretching, yawning, and scractching his side.

"Merry Christmas, Grandpa," Tina said.

"Merry Christmas, baby—all my babies."

Brianna got up and bustled over to the hot plate. "How's

special Christmas pancakes sound to everybody?" she asked cheerily.

"How're they any different from the pancakes we have every day?" Jamie asked.

"Well, I'm fixin' 'em on Christmas but—"

Just then there was a loud knocking at the door. Grandpa answered it, peeking in the little glass eye first to see who it was. He turned around and said in a scared voice, "It's Ms. Banks."

"Stop fooling, Dad. You're scaring the kids," Mama told him.

"No, it's really her," he said.

The pounding increased and Ms. Banks's unmistakable voice called, "Mr. Timmons, do you intend for me to spend this entire holiday banging on your door or will you for Pete's sake let me in?"

Grandpa shrugged, unfastened the chain, and let her in. A man stood beside her holding a computer. Tina's heart sank. Had she broken it accidentally?

"Mr. Timmons, if I may enter?" Ms. Banks said, all stiff and formal and mad-like.

"Surely you may, Ms. Banks. Merry Christmas. You, too, Curtis."

The man who held the computer gave Grandpa a stiff little nod.

"Won't you . . . sit here, Ms. Banks?" Grandpa asked, motioning to his own chair, which nobody ever sat in but him.

"Thank you, I prefer to stand to say to you what I've got

to say. Mr. Timmons, it has come to my attention that you have a granddaughter—"

"Y-yes, ma'am, this is Tina."

"And that you have been bringing this child to work with you where she has been messing around with computers."

"I didn't know about that until last night, ma'am. See, I have to bring Tina to work with me when Tiffany is working nights. Tiffany's my oldest girl there, and that's Brianna, my next girl, and Jamie, my boy. But Tina's heart doesn't work so good and—"

Grandpa looked like he was about to cry. Tina was about to yell at Ms. Banks not to be so mean when the lady broke into a big grin.

"On the contrary, Mr. Timmons, Tina's heart works very well indeed. One of the best I've ever seen. Any small mechanical problems that require medical attention will be dealt with by the very best doctors as soon as we can arrange it. As for the computer, since she's already familiar with this one, I thought she should have it to learn on. Since she may have to take time out for her surgeries, I thought she ought to start before the other students."

"I'm darned if I know what you're talking about, Ms. Banks."

"Time to drop the high-handed thing now, maybe, Monica," Curtis said with a big grin, which Ms. Banks, of all things, returned. "Don't want to put Noah's back up or he might not let his kids anywhere near your new project—"

"But he has to, Curtis!" Ms. Banks said as if she was

really upset. "Unless Noah agrees to take the job, I can't possibly keep that building running—"

"What job?" Grandpa asked.

"Can I set this thing down?" Curtis asked. Brianna cleared the table off for him and Jamie helped him plug it in. Then Curtis left.

"Wait!" Grandpa tried to stop him, as if he was still afraid to be with Ms. Banks. "Where you going?"

"He just went to get the software," Ms. Banks said. "Now, as to the job. I want to . . . that is, my associates and I . . . and by the way, you are as of this Christmas a stockholder in Databanks, but I still have to have the legal papers drawn up, as soon as I've retained a new attorney to fire my old ones.

"Anyway, as I was saying, my brother's house is really too big and kind of inhuman for me. But it's an enormous house with nice grounds, and I thought perhaps it would make an adequate school. The only problem is, the whole thing is electronically run and not just anyone could manage it. But I happen to value you as an extremely conscientious and caring employee, and I would like to hire you away from the subcontractor you've been working for, have you train with one of the experts who installed Doug's system, and learn to run the house. Then I want to turn it into a sort of a technical prep school for people of all ages who need work and training for work. Like your granddaughter and your children there.

"Of course, I can't have the children unsupervised in that

large, complicated house, and you will be busy with your duties, so I'm delighted to see you have an adult daughter."

She turned to Tiffany. "I wonder if you might be willing to train with us, too, Tiffany. At first, I could only offer you half of what I would one of the teachers to supervise the children, but if it works out, we could get you further training and you could either remain with them as an instructor or go on to some occupation of your own choosing, though of course we hope you'd look at Databanks first."

"Ms. Banks, I'm overwhelmed, I really don't know what to say," Grandpa said.

Ms. Banks said, "I've got another favor to ask you, Mr. Timmons. I got this great big ham as a Christmas present with all the fixings, and I'm way too busy today to fix it. I'd feel so relieved about the waste if your family could take it for me."

"Yes, *ma'am,*" Brianna said, rubbing her hands together.

"It's in a basket in the hall," Ms. Banks said. "Oh, one more thing. I hope you won't think it too personal, but since I don't have a family anymore, I thought I'd bring a few gifts for yours."

At that moment, a lady appeared at the door with several wrapped presents in her hands as Curtis reappeared.

"Ms. Banks, we can't take presents from you," Grandpa said. "You've done so much already. I can't believe this is real—"

"I should have done it a long time ago," she said. "I'm catching up on a lot of things today. But go on, take them, it's not much really—"

"Monica," the lady in the door said. "While I was out getting the presents, I stopped by the pound to give Bonita your donation like you asked, and she had just found this on the doorstep."

"Let's have a look," she said and brought the box over to the window where Tina was. "Tina, if I open this, will you please remove the contents?"

Tina nodded gravely and Ms. Banks opened the lid. Tina had to lean over quite a ways to see into the box, but when she did, tiny white paws stretched up to meet her. It was the most beautiful little green-eyed, fluffy, yellow kitten she'd ever seen. "Oh, he's beeoooteeful. What's his name?"

"I don't know. He's an orphan, I guess. You want him?"

"I'm sorry, Ms. Banks . . . and Tina, honey, but you know we can't have pets in this building."

"You can now," Monica said. "I called the realtor this morning. Your landlord had been meaning to sell in order to turn it into condos. I prefer the rental market myself, but I do need to protect my investment, so there'll be some changes made around here very soon. However, in the meantime, I do allow Christmas kittens in my building."

"You've been a busy woman, Ms. Banks."

Ms. Banks grinned and followed Curtis and the pretty lady out the door. "You betcha, Mr. Timmons. Merry Christmas, everyone. Please report to Databanks tomorrow long enough to pick up your paycheck from your former employer, Mr. Timmons. I think you'll find it quite sufficient to tide you over until after the New Year when your new job begins."

"Merry Christmas, Ms. Banks," he said, and so did Tiffany and Jamie and Brianna. Tina, cuddling the kitten, used the furniture to make her way to the door to watch Ms. Banks go, too.

"Merry Christmas!" she called down the steps after the lady. She leaned against her grandpa and waved with one hand while making the kitty's paw wave with the other, "From me and Scroogie!"

Seventeen

ᏪᎷᎡᏅ

Monica left Curtis and Melody at the curb. "I've given all the authorizations. All of our other donations will be kept anonymous, okay?"

"Okay, Monica," both Curtis and Melody said.

"The others know what to do and where to go, too. Now, I want you guys to go skiing or something while I'm gone. We'll sort out the legal thing later."

"Monica, my mom's like this really top attorney, except you probably never heard of her 'cause she's, like, a liberal?" Melody said.

"Give her my cell-phone number. And be sure and watch the news for Bambi Billings's scoop about what good old Bob intended our Get a Life program to do on the side so the consumers will know why it's not coming out as scheduled—"

"You know, Monica, it was really cool how Buddha-like you were with Jamie and Billings and the house and all," Curtis said. "Turning the other cheek and everything. I've been thinking about a replacement product. What about maybe a Holiday-Maker—"

"With a vastly comprehensive shopping feature that plugs in local small businesses as well as malls and catalogs and TV options—" Melody added.

"As well as folklore, customs, cross-referencing the teachings of various religious and secular leaders, and a list of organizations and causes that need help locally, nationally, and internationally, plus maybe parties for people with different interests to celebrate together—"

"That's work," Monica said sternly.

"But programming is my life!" Curtis protested.

"So have fun," Monica said, ducking into her car. "But Curtis, I do like it."

She saw him beaming through her rearview mirror as she drove away. Both he and Melody were waving and yelling, "Merry Christmas." She waved and yelled back.

Wayne threw a robe around himself and answered the door. He almost fell over when he saw Monica standing there, wearing a smart trench coat and bearing a fruitcake. "Hi, Wayne. I came to spend Christmas with you like you keep asking me to, okay?"

"M-Monica. But . . . you said—"

"A lady can change her mind, can't she?"

"Yeah, but—"

"But?"

"Nice trench coat."

"Thanks. I got it at Nordstrom's this morning along with a few other things. I can show you later. You're not even dressed."

"I wasn't expecting you. You've only been turning me down for twenty years."

"Well, I'm not turning you down now," she said. "But hurry. We have to get on the road right away."

"On the road?" he asked.

"The snow has cleared down south and we can make it to Portland in time if we hurry."

"In time for what?"

"To catch a plane to Florida, silly." She loosened the neck of her trench coat and pulled out a little bit of lace. "I'm wearing your mom's collar. Think it might bring back some memories?"

"Oops, watch out! Major mistletoe attack!" he said and swept her up in a big hug, kissed her the way he'd always wanted to, and waited for her to reject him.

"What mistletoe?" she mumbled.

"It's virtual mistletoe," he whispered into her hair.

"Oh, okay then." She kissed him back and grinned. "Watch out what you ask for, they say. You just might get it. Coming?"

"On my way. What happens if we don't outrun the snow in Portland?"

"We keep driving till we hit an open airport or Florida, whichever comes first."

"You've gone nuts. We'll have to get you into therapy when we get back, of course, but right now, I'm just going to enjoy it."

A few minutes later, they were driving in a winter wonderland, agreeing that it was a good thing they were rich enough that they didn't have to pack.

Epilogue

⌒⊸

The Get a Life team met, as they'd arranged among themselves, back at their own cold, empty Databanks building at the end of Christmas day. By mutual agreement, they entered the building and made their way to Curtis's office.

"That's everything then?" Curtis asked.

"Yeah," John said with relish. "I accomplished the liberation of Mrs. Johansen's cat, reunited her with the kittens Melody got from Bonita, and they're staying at my place till Wayne and Monica get back."

"Cool."

Then Sheryl said what everyone else had been thinking since Curtis and Melody contacted them earlier. "We need to get this project up and ready with a big bow around it by the time Monica gets back, or this big shopping spree is going to be her last one before she loses her butt. *Our* butts. So, okay, Curtis, boot up and let's get started mapping it out."

He turned on his machine, only to find it filled with static snow. He was just starting to fear something was wrong with it, when the familiar face of Ebenezer Scrooge appeared on the screen.

"Of course, he'd be wanting a report. Hey, Scrooge, everything's great. You made a real human being out of the boss, and I think it's going to be a lot different around here."

"I'm so glad," Scrooge said. "The Program Manager seems pleased, but I can't help feeling sorry that all of you still have so many problems—with the shopping and the commercialization and that sort of thing—enjoying Christmas."

"Think nothing of it, Scrooge," Miriam said, kissing her fingers, and laying them against his face on the screen. "With you around to entertain me, it's been a better Christmas than I've ever had and December twenty-fifth will never pass again without me thinking about this one."

"Me, neither," Curtis said, and all of the others seemed to concur. "Everyone in this business with an ounce of imagination and a background of reading too much pulp science fiction as a kid dreams that one day computers will come to life and take over, and you showed us something as close to that as I ever hope to come. It was a rush, man."

From all around him came nods of agreement. Scrooge noticed, incidentally, that Melody now stood much closer to Curtis than she had before, that Harald and Miriam were holding hands, and John and Sheryl were exchanging glances.

"But, Ebbie, just one thing," Melody said. "Now that you're, like, finished here, do you have to go back to being dead again?"

"Oh, my dear young lady, it's not so bad as everyone

seems to think, you know. But as a matter of fact, the Program Manager was sufficiently impressed with my—I should really say our, since you were of so much assistance to me with the morphing and everything—performance, that he wishes me to do an encore. I believe our Monica's departed brother is also to be a part of the festivities, since he was also acquainted with the new . . . er . . . subject."

"Really? But Christmas is nearly over."

"Not for me, my dear. Never for me," Scrooge said. "I seem to have—ahem—developed a knack for time travel. Now if you'll excuse me, I must board a flight for Hong Kong, last night when Christmas had yet to spread its wings over the world."

He vanished with a last tip of his top hat, leaving his friends to enjoy their holidays, as indeed they did.

Starting with that Christmas, and on all of the Christmases to follow, Monica Banks was better than her word. She did it all, and more. She was like a second mother to Tina, who did not die but lived to become one of the most brilliant programmers and cybernauts in the history of technology. Her family fared equally well, as did the many other people throughout the city that Monica's new school and Databanks benefitted. She did not queen it over everyone, but became the best friend, the best boss, and the best woman in Seattle or any other city, town, or county in the world, as Wayne was fond of telling her.

Under her leadership, Databanks, in association with Wild Web, was known nationwide and worldwide as an example of the New American Corporation—the company with a heart. At first, the press laughed at Monica and said that she had merely changed image consultants, but she, Wayne, and her former employees, now new associates, just laughed with them and said people could use a good laugh these days. Their happiness spread, not like ripples in a still pond but more like oil (nonpolluting, of course) soothing the troubled waters of a wider and wider population as it touched every product the company designed. The new line began with the World of Christmas and added more products with such wit, intelligence, good humor, and creativity in their design that new offerings from Databanks, at affordable prices and with excellent consumer support, were soon even more eagerly awaited than the latest ice cream from the beneficent ice cream company or the salad dressings from movie stars.

The press laughed even harder when Monica Banks paid not only her fair share of taxes, but a bit more because, as she said, why should the poor bear the brunt of the taxes? She would prefer they had a bit more to buy the products her company had designed to improve their lives.

Although she had no further close encounters with spirits, staying on the wagon where they were concerned ever afterward, it was always said of her that Monica Banks was the woman who knew how to make Christmas merry, and the season happy if anyone alive did. And so, as Tina put it every year, quoting Tiny Tim, with whom she had much in common, "God bless us, every one."